Friends Forever
Baby-sitters Club

(Graduation Day)

Ann M. Martin

AN
APPLE
PAPERBACK

SCHOLASTIC INC.
New York   Toronto   London   Auckland   Sydney
Mexico City   New Delhi   Hong Kong

*For all the readers — past, present, and future —
of the Baby-sitters Club books . . . with thanks.*

*If you purchased this book without a cover, you should be aware that this
book is stolen property. It was reported as "unsold and destroyed" to the
publisher, and neither the author nor the publisher has received any payment
for this "stripped book."*

No part of this publication may be reproduced in whole or in part, or stored
in a retrieval system or transmitted in any form or by any means, electronic,
mechanical, photocopying, recording, or otherwise, without written permission of the publisher. For information regarding permission, write to Scholastic Inc., Attention: Permissions Department, 555 Broadway, New York,
NY 10012.

ISBN 0-439-21918-3

Copyright © 2000 by Ann M. Martin. All rights reserved. Published by
Scholastic Inc. SCHOLASTIC, THE BABY-SITTERS CLUB, APPLE PAPER-
BACKS, and associated logos are trademarks and/or registered trademarks of
Scholastic Inc.

12 11 10 9 8 7 6 5 4 3 2 1   0/0 1 2 3 4 5/0

Printed in the U.S.A.   40

First Scholastic printing, November 2000

❀ Kristy

may 31

Can't believe am about to graduate. Definitely not ready for it. Possible to graduate from 8th grade, then return to SMS and have a do-over? Am REALLY not ready for high school. Tried to explain this to Mom. Was told am being silly. According to Mom, all freshmen are nervous about starting high school. Since when does Mom consider her dear daughter like everyone else?

Walked through the halls of SMS today and was BOMBARDED by notices about caps and gowns, yearbooks, and like. Every notice frightening. How am I supposed to concentrate on finals with all these distractions? Oh! Maybe if flunk finals will have to repeat 8th grade. Good idea.

Note to self: Ask Charlie if he felt like this when he was leaving SMS. . . .

It was a very hot night — hot for May, that is — and I was lying in my bedroom with the windows open, listening to the late spring nighttime sounds. I'm pretty sure I was the only one in my whole house who was still awake. And with a family my size, that is saying a lot. All around me were bedrooms with sleeping people in them. My mom and Watson in one. (Watson is my stepfather. He's pretty cool, even if he is going bald.) My big brother Charlie in one; my other big brother, Sam, in one; my little brother David Michael in one; my little sister Karen in one; my little brother Andrew in one; my little sister Emily Michelle in one; and my grandmother Nannie in one. And all of them asleep, as far as I knew.

Just me awake and stewing. For three years my friends and I have been edging our way through SMS, or Stoneybrook Middle School. And now, after three years of projects, tests, report cards, field trips, cafeteria meals, softball games, and dances, it's about to end. We are about to graduate and go on to SHS, Stoneybrook High School. That's where my brothers Sam and Charlie are students. Sam will be a junior

next year, and Charlie is going off to *col...*
we're pretty sure he's going off to college. Cha...
a very un-Charlie sort of thing this year. For on...
his life he wasn't all organized and on top of things.
He didn't get around to applying to colleges until it
was on the late side. Charlie is a really good student
and could probably go to just about any college — if
he had applied on time. But he dropped the ball
(Watson's words), and even after a lot of prodding
from Mom and Watson, his applications were out
too late to qualify for the top schools. He's waiting
now to hear from a few small local ones. He says he
wants to go to Boiceville State. We'll see.

Anyway, I do not understand why we should
turn our nice lives topsy-turvy. Everything has been
quite fine in the last year or so. Everyone in my
whole family (my WHOLE family, Charlie) is settled
where they belong. But in the fall so much is going to
change. Sam and I will be the high school students.
David Michael and Karen, who are seven, will just
stay in their schools and move on to third grade, but
Andrew will start kindergarten, and Emily Michelle
will start full-time preschool. (In case you're wondering about my enormous family, Karen and Andrew
are actually my stepsister and stepbrother. They're
Watson's kids from his first marriage.)

Here's the thing. I'm a firm believer that if something isn't broken, you shouldn't fix it. (Or as Watson would say, "If it ain't broke, don't fix it.") And I kind of like things the way they are right now. I'm worried that once my friends and I get to high school, our friendships are going to change. There will be SO MANY kids at SHS. It's a much bigger school than the middle school. Kids come to SHS from *all* the middle schools in Stoneybrook as well as middle schools from a couple of other towns. There will be over a THOUSAND kids at SHS. I bet I could go all day there without seeing Claudia or Stacey or Mary Anne. Anyway, they'll be off making new friends, which they'll have to do, because they won't be able to find one another or me in the maze of corridors and rooms that make up SHS.

And then there's the Baby-sitters Club, or BSC. The BSC is really a business (a baby-sitting business, as if you couldn't guess) started by yours truly almost two years ago, at the beginning of seventh grade. All my closest friends belong to it. At one time it was a really big deal. Seven of us belonged as full-fledged members, with various honorary and associate members.

Now the club has scaled back to the original four

members (Mary Anne, Claudia, Stacey, and me), but it's still important to us. We meet several times a week to assign sitting jobs, to discuss our clients and the jobs we've been on, and also just to talk, to catch up, to be together. Are we really going to be able to continue this once we start high school? We're going to be so much busier. For one thing, we'll be in school until later in the afternoon. Then there will be all the extra work and so many after-school clubs, teams, and activities. I have a funny feeling the four of us may not wind up meeting very often.

And I can't bear to think about not spending so much time with my friends, not seeing the little kids we've all grown close to. . . .

Take today. Today was a very typical, very good day. In the morning, Charlie drove himself and Sam to school in his car, the Junk Bucket. David Michael, Karen, and I went off to school on our various buses, and Emily waved good-bye to us from the front door, where she was standing with Nannie. Mom was about to leave for her job, and Watson was already at work in his office at home. At school I met up with Mary Anne, Claudia, Abby, and Jessi at my locker. (Abby and Jessi are former BSC members who are still our close friends.) We chatted until the bell rang for homeroom. At lunch, I sat with Stacey, Abby, Mary Anne, and Claudia. We always grab the same table. There is nothing like knowing where you're going to sit at lunch and who you'll sit with. None of that embarrassing wandering around with a tray, wondering if you'll be welcome at a table of strangers. We picked up practically in the middle of a sentence, finishing up a conversation we had started in the morning.

After school I walked with Claudia to her neighborhood, because I was going to baby-sit for Jamie and Lucy Newton. I took Jamie and Lucy to the playground — and there was Stacey with Charlotte Johanssen. A few minutes later, Mary Anne showed up with two of the Rodowsky boys. We organized the kids into a game of dodgeball. (Lucy watched from her stroller.) When our various sitting jobs were over we gathered at Claudia's house for a BSC meeting. The only bad part of this whole wonderful normal day was that at the meeting my friends couldn't stop talking about graduation.

"Did you see the notice about picking up our caps and gowns?" Stacey said. "Oh, I can't wait. I'm going to try mine on as soon as I have it."

"Isn't that bad luck or something?" I said. "No

one is supposed to see us in our caps and gowns before we graduate."

"The *groom* isn't supposed to see the *bride* in her wedding gown before the wedding," said Claudia. "No one cares about caps and gowns."

"Oh," I said.

"Hey," spoke up Mary Anne, "did you see? They already posted the list of times when we can take a tour of the high school. I'm going to sign up right away."

"Me too," said Stacey.

"Me three." Claudia stuffed a handful of popcorn in her mouth. "I hee ray hab a wait at zubio rare."

"What?" I said.

Claudia swallowed. "I hear they have a great art studio there."

Couldn't anyone talk about anything else?

Luckily the phone rang then. Mrs. Prezzioso needed a sitter. We turned our attention back to the meeting.

Yes, except for that conversation at the meeting, today had been a wonderful day. I pretty much knew what to expect from it. I had seen my friends, my family, some of our sitting charges. I had been to a school I knew my way around. I had attended a BSC meeting. And now I was in bed with my family close by.

So why couldn't I sleep?

I couldn't sleep because I didn't want any of it to end.

Mary Anne

Thursday, June 1

Dear Diary,

Hi. I'm back. We had such an exciting day at school! Everywhere there are signs of graduation and all the end-of-the-year stuff. We're going to get our yearbooks in about two weeks. And I know it was kind of silly, but I signed up to get one of those memory boxes to keep all my special memorabilia in — graduation cards and *so forth. The boxes are going to be handed out next week.*

Best of all was the assembly. It was just for us graduating eighth-graders...

I can't explain how excited I am about graduation. I don't know why. Maybe because of what graduation represents. Three years of hard work and the fact that our teachers and parents think we're ready to move on to high school. We're taking a giant step forward, and the grown-ups are standing on the sidelines, cheering us on, saying we can do it, maybe even that they expect great things from us. Some people might find this intimidating, but not me. I feel ready.

At dinner tonight Dad said to me, "Mary Anne, you seem awfully happy."

"I am." I grinned at him and Sharon, and they grinned back.

I was looking around the kitchen in our new house. At first I had thought I might not like making the switch from an old house (a *really* old house) to a new one. A brand-new one. It was completed just a few months ago, after the old one had burned to the ground. Actually, the big barn that was on our property was converted into this new house. Everything in it is new — all the furniture, all the appliances, everything hanging on the walls, every item in every drawer. All of it bought recently. I had been afraid I wouldn't like it, but I do. I like the freshness of it. It feels like a new start. And so does high school. New starts are very appealing now.

"Good day at school?" asked Sharon.

Sharon is my stepmother. We get along well, considering the beginning of our relationship wasn't very smooth. But Sharon is the only mother I've known, and now that we're used to each other, I'm glad she's a part of my life. I can talk to her about things I can't discuss with my father. It's sort of like having a good friend living right in my home.

"Very good day at school," I replied.

"So tell," said Sharon with a smile.

"Well, we had an assembly this morning, and Mr. Kingbridge told us about this letter project."

"Ah," said Dad, and a fond, faraway look came into his eyes as he remembered when he was an SMS student. "So they're still doing that? I remember my letter. Do you remember yours, Sharon?"

"Of course," she replied. (She had gone to school with Dad.)

I thought back to school that morning. We hadn't known we were going to have an assembly. The news was sprung on us during homeroom. I love when morning announcements are actually interesting or surprising, as opposed to an announcement about a change in the lunch menu or some green Plymouth's headlights having been left on in the south parking lot.

My teacher had just finished taking attendance when I heard the PA system come on. Soon Mr. Kingbridge's voice was telling the eighth-graders to gather in the auditorium at the beginning of fourth period. (Mr. Kingbridge is our vice-principal.)

"Yes!" I heard someone say beneath his breath from the row behind me.

Mr. Kingbridge had sounded sort of pleased with himself, so I figured this wasn't an announcement about final exams or some other horrible thing.

When the bell rang at the end of third period I rushed out of my classroom and hurried down the hall to Kristy's locker. She was standing in front of it with Claudia.

"Let's go," I said.

Kristy was moving in slow motion, rearranging things in her locker. "Just a minute."

"No, come on. This is going to be good," I said. "I know it."

Claudia and I dragged Kristy away from her locker and we sped through the halls. We passed under a banner announcing GRADUATION BALL — EIGHTH-GRADE DANCE. We hurried by the bulletin board outside the office, which is usually covered in memos and notices, but today said simply, CONGRAT- ULATIONS, GRADUATES!!

"We haven't even graduated yet," Kristy complained.

"It's only three weeks from now," I replied, feeling a little thrill wash over me.

We ran into the auditorium and grabbed five seats near the front.

"Where are Stacey and Abby?" asked Claudia.

"There they are," I said. I waved to them and they ran for the seats we were saving.

At that moment Mr. Kingbridge stepped onto the stage. He didn't waste any time. "As some of you may know," he said, "for decades it has been a tradi- tion here at Stoneybrook Middle School for each of you eighth-graders to write a letter to yourself — a

13

letter that will be mailed *back* to you in four years, when you are graduating from high school." I heard uncertain murmurs around me. "Your letter," Mr. Kingbridge went on, "should be like a small personal time capsule. I suggest you write about anything that seems to capture you as you are today, and also about what you think you might be doing in four years, apart from graduating again. Think about events in your lives that you feel have *defined* you. Think about what is important to you now, about the things that have had an impact on you and about your hopes and dreams for the future. Believe me, your letter will be very interesting when it is mailed back to you in four years.

"Writing your letter, by the way," Mr. Kingbridge continued, "is not mandatory. You are not required to write one. And your letter will not affect your grades in any way. This is simply a fun SMS tradition. So if you are interested, think about your letter and start to write it. Give it to me anytime during the next two weeks, and I will hold on to it for four years. Any questions?"

I didn't listen to the questions. I was already thinking about my letter. Defining events. My dreams for the future. Wow. Where would I begin? So many things seemed to be defining. And my dreams for the future? To be honest, I hadn't thought much beyond starting high school. I wasn't even sure what I wanted to be. I wished I were like Claudia, who has known practically forever that one day she will be an artist.

When the assembly ended I stood up and looked at my friends. "Are you guys going to write letters?" I asked them.

"Yup," they all replied. Even Claudia. I hadn't thought she would write one. Writing anything is a chore for her.

"I kind of remember when Charlie wrote his," added Kristy. "He was holed up in his bedroom for, like, three nights. I thought he was studying for finals, and it turned out he was writing this letter. Now he'll be getting it back soon."

"Cool," I said, even though I really couldn't imagine being Charlie's age, getting ready for college, waiting for my letter to arrive. It just didn't seem possible.

Abby nudged me as we were edging our way up the aisle toward the back of the auditorium. "Logan," she whispered.

He had materialized next to me with a pack of

his friends. I glanced at him. He glanced at me. We did not speak. We have barely exchanged two words since we broke up. And that was how I wanted it.

Wasn't it?

In truth, it wasn't a very nice way to behave around someone I thought had played a defining role in my life. And even though it seemed Logan and I had talked endlessly about our relationship, our friendship, what we meant to each other, what had gone wrong — something felt unfinished. Something about *us* felt unfinished. And I didn't like that.

Still, the very thought of writing my special letter made me smile. And that feeling of contentment stuck with me until the end of the day.

Stacey

From: NYCGirl
Subject: Caps & Gowns
To: bigdad
Date: Friday, June 2
Time: 9:48:21 P.M.

Hi, Dad!
 How's everything going?
 I was thinking of you today because we had to measure our heads for our graduation caps, and then I began to imagine you at graduation. Can you believe that we had to <u>measure our heads</u>? Each 8th-grader was supposed to drop by the gym at some point today, and we were given a measuring tape and a form to fill out.
 I had a BSC meeting this afternoon after I

baby-sat for Charlotte again, so it was a busy day.

Anyway, I just wanted to tell you about the caps. I'm getting excited about graduation. Can't wait to see you! Say hi to Samantha.

Love, Stacey

Hmm. If I could change one thing about graduation it would be the fact that both of my parents are going to be there. Not that I don't want both of them there, but, well, maybe we could have two separate graduations. I can't possibly be the only eighth-grader with divorced parents who would rather not be in the same audience at the same time. In fact, as far as I can tell, my parents would rather not be in the same town at the same time. If Kristy's father lived here instead of in California, I bet Kristy would want separate graduations too.

Oh, well. I'm just being silly. I mean, this is our *graduation*. It's one of the more exciting things that's ever happened to me. A cap, a gown, a diploma, and on to high school. The big league.

That's what I was thinking about while I waited for our BSC meeting to begin this afternoon. I was looking around at Kristy and Claudia and Claudia's bedroom while we waited for Mary Anne to show up. I was thinking about how many, many meetings we've held there in the past couple of years. And I was watching Claud dig a bag of jelly beans out from the back of her desk drawer, while Kristy doodled on the palm of her hand with a Magic Marker. Then I thought of high school and the big league. The Big League. I wondered how many BSC meetings we'd hold once school started again in September. The BSC was seeming sort of minor league compared to SHS.

It was a small mean thought, but there it was in my head.

I pushed it away.

Because the BSC is where I found all my best friends when I first moved to Stoneybrook. I will admit that Claud and I have had some bad times, friendship-wise. Still . . . Claudia, Kristy, Mary Anne, Jessi, Mallory, Abby, Dawn. We were brought together by the BSC. And a lot of memories have been created because of the BSC.

Maybe it isn't so minor league after all.

Kristy was just completing her hand-doodle, which had turned into a dragon, when Mary Anne burst through the door and flung herself onto the bed.

"Sorry, sorry, sorry," she said. "Am I late?" She

looked at Claud's clock. Then she grinned smugly. "Five twenty-nine," she announced. "Safe."

Kristy put down the green marker. "Close call," she said. "Okay. This meeting of the Baby-sitters Club will now come to order. Any new business?"

"You mean baby-sitting business?" asked Claudia. "Because if not, can I just say that my graduation cap — "

She stopped speaking when she saw Kristy giving her a Look from the director's chair, where she was perched with a pencil over one ear. "Yes, I mean baby-sitting business," said Kristy. She looked around at each of us.

To tell the truth, as much as I LOVE the BSC, as many things as it's brought me, as much fun as I've had being a part of it . . . I know it is more important to Kristy than it is to me or to any of the rest of us. And Kristy looked so earnest now, in her chair with the pencil over her ear, a notebook open in her lap, that I tried desperately to think of something that might qualify as new baby-sitting business.

"Um," I said, thinking, "um, you should all know that . . . that Charlotte is going to get an award at her end-of-school assembly." (This was true, and it wasn't bad, as club business goes.) "It's a writing award, and she's really proud, but she's too shy to say anything. Um, Dr. Johanssen told me so I could congratulate Charlotte, and you guys might want to congratulate her too. Since she won't tell you about it herself."

"A writing award. Very cool," said Mary Anne.

"Definitely," Kristy agreed.

"Can you believe that Charlotte will be in fourth grade next year?" Claud asked.

"The kids we've been baby-sitting for are growing up so fast!" exclaimed Mary Anne.

"You sound like my mother," I said. "When she's talking about me."

"Can we get back to club busi — " Kristy was saying when the phone rang. She grabbed it. "Hello, Baby-sitters Club," she said. "Oh, hi, Mrs. Pike. . . . Monday? This Monday? . . . That's not such short notice. Don't worry. Let me call you right back. Mary Anne will check our schedule."

By the time Kristy had hung up the phone, Mary Anne had opened our club record book and was checking the appointment pages. "What time Monday?" she asked Kristy.

"Right after school. It's for all the Pikes, but Mal will be home to be the other sitter."

There are so many Pike kids — eight, including Mallory, who's the oldest and an honorary BSC

21

member — that we need two sitters at their house if we're going to baby-sit for all her brothers and sisters. We don't feel comfortable with just one sitter for more than four kids. This is one of the many sensible BSC rules that Kristy has insisted upon.

It was great to have Mal around again. She now goes to a private school in Massachusetts, but her school term had already ended, and she was home for the summer.

"Actually," said Mary Anne, "it looks like I'm the only one free. Mal and I can take the job together."

"Great," Kristy said, and phoned Mrs. Pike back.

A few other calls came in before the meeting ended. Once upon a time, when my friends and I were a little younger, a little more into baby-sitting, and a little less busy with sports and other activities, the BSC was a much bigger deal. We had more members because we needed them. Sitting jobs were called in almost as fast as we could fill them. The pace has slowed since we scaled the club back awhile ago, and I have to admit I'm relieved. I don't think Kristy is, though. I think she misses it.

The numbers on Claudia's clock flipped over to 6:00, and Mary Anne, Kristy, and I stood up.

"Want to stay for dinner?" Claud asked me as I was about to leave.

"Sure."

It was a nice, simple invitation — one that in the past I wouldn't have thought twice about, because it would have been so normal. Now I marveled at its normalcy. Every day that passed meant we were a little farther from our big fight and closer to the way our friendship used to be.

I was glad. I didn't want to graduate from SMS with any bad feelings about my friends.

Claudia

June 3 7:38:52 P.M.
INSTANT MESSAGE

CKishi: Hey stace whats going on.
NYCGirl: Hi, Claud! Just checking my e-mail. What are you doing?
CKishi: Your going to think I'm crazy starting a assinment on sat. night but I decided to start my letter to myslef.
NYCGirl: Great! How's it going?
CKishi: Its hard!!!!! Have you started yours yet.
NYCGirl: Not yet. Just thinking about it.
CKishi: I was porcri prok prokras putting mine off by reading my e-mail but I guess I'll go back to it now
NYCGirl: Ciao, then. Later.
CKishi: Later

Why was it so hard to write a letter to myself? It was a perfectly good Saturday night, one with a lot of excellent TV shows that I had been planning to watch as soon as I had written down a few ideas for my letter. But the hours were slipping by and I still had no idea where my letter was going. (The best of the TV shows had already ended.)

I had started by making a list of people who are or who have been important to me. Mom, Dad, Janine, Mimi, Peaches, Russ, Lynn, Kristy, Stacey, Mary Anne, Dawn, Jessi, Abby, Mal, Alan, Jamie and Lucy Newton . . . This was nice, but I wasn't sure what to do with it. Plus, the list was getting out of hand. I had included Peaches, Russ, and Lynn. Should I add the rest of my relatives too? Alan made me think of past boyfriends and I wondered whether to put all of them down. The Newton kids made me think of the rest of our sitting charges, and I actually *did* start to list them, then realized how long the list was getting. I hadn't even written down the names of my art teachers or of artists I admire.

I threw the list of people away and started writing down important events in my life. There was Mimi's funeral; the day Lynn was born; the day I met Stacey; my big fight with Stacey; my first art class; the day I was told I would have to repeat seventh grade; my sixth birthday party, when the guests didn't show up; and the time I went to the beach with Kristy's family and lost David Michael. But were any of these *defining* events? (What exactly was a defining event?)

I threw the list of events away too and turned my thoughts back to the people in my family. My mom and dad. My sister, Janine. Hmm. Janine is a genius. I have grown up with a genius (while I am far from a genius myself, at least where schoolwork is concerned). Is that defining? Then, of course, there is Mimi. My wonderful grandmother. I had been as close to Mimi as I was to anyone else in my family — to anyone else in the world. And then she was gone. I still miss Mimi. I miss her every day. In the very beginning, just after she died, I couldn't even figure out how *not* to think about her. Finally, I began working on a portrait of her, and I found other ways to keep her memory in my life without being overtaken by sadness. So Mimi's death was definitely a defining event.

"Dear Me," I wrote. Well, that sounded awfully funny. "Dear You," I tried. And then, "Dear Claudia."

Okay. I had the beginning of my letter.

Great. I had been sitting in my room for two

hours, missing good TV shows, and all I had come up with was "Dear Claudia." Anyone could have written that.

My mind wandered. Maybe my phone would ring. A little chat with Stacey might perk me up. Funny. A year ago a little chat with Stacey would definitely have perked me up. I wouldn't even have had to think about it. But Stacey and I are still dancing around each other a little, just the teensiest bit uncertain about our friendship. I mean, the friendship is still there, but it has changed. I hate to say this, but I feel as if I don't trust her one hundred percent anymore. And I can't believe that the reason we had a fight in the first place was over a boy. But it did happen.

Speaking of boys, maybe Alan would call. Alan can always make me laugh. It's such a shame that the rest of my friends don't like him much. I do understand that he's been a major pain since forever (I used to be one of the ones who thought he was a major pain), but he really isn't like that anymore. At least not around me.

Hmm. I wonder if in four years Alan and I will still be going out. Four years sounds like a lot of time to go out with the same person. In four years I'll be almost eighteen. On the other hand, I've been friends with some people for a lot longer than four years. Now, why is it that four years sounds long when I'm thinking in terms of Alan Gray, but not so long when I'm thinking in terms of Kristy or Mary Anne?

I turned back to my letter. I changed the font on my computer and wrote ``Dear Claudia´´ instead.

Okay. Good job, Claud.

I had basically accomplished nothing.

At long last, the phone actually rang.

"Hello?" I said.

Kristy used to make me answer my phone, "Hello, Baby-sitters Club," even when we weren't having a meeting, but I had finally told her that I wasn't going to do that anymore. I have a feeling that when I get to SHS next fall I probably will answer the phone in a whole new way.

When I get to SHS? Let's face it, I mean, IF I get to SHS. I am hanging on to eighth grade by a thread. I have JUST managed to make it this far. I have gone back to seventh grade, worked with tutors, spent countless hours in the resource room, and I'm not sure what will happen if I don't pass all my final exams.

"Hello?" I said again when I heard nothing on the other end of the phone.

"Um . . . is this Elio's?"

"Elio's?" I repeated.

"Sorry, I think I have the wrong number." Clunk. The caller hung up.

I looked at my pitiful letter to myself. Then I looked at the stack of books and papers that I should have been studying in order to pass my exams.

If I flunked and had to spend another year at SMS while my friends went on to SHS, I would . . . I would . . . Well, I wasn't sure what I would do, but it wouldn't be anything good.

✸ Mary Anne

Monday, June 5

Dear Diary,

Mal and I baby-sat
together at her house
this afternoon. We
haven't done that in
awhile, and it was
really fun. I miss Mallory.
I'm glad she's so much
happier at her new
school, but I do miss
her.

This afternoon was like
old times. All Mal's
brothers and sisters
were around. The triplets
don't need much looking

after anymore, but since it was a rainy day, the nine of us were cooped up inside, and the kids were starting to get stir-crazy. To distract them, I told them about our letter-writing project...

"Mary Anne!" shrieked Claire at the top of her lungs when she answered my knock at the Pikes' door. She sounded as if she hadn't seen me in years.

"Hi, Claire," I replied. I tried to take off my drippy coat and boots without leaving puddles in the Pikes' front hallway. "Maybe I should stick these back outside," I said.

"No, they'll get all wet."

I looked at Claire. "They're already all wet," I pointed out.

"Oh, yeah."

Mal appeared. "Hi, Mary Anne. Put your boots on this newspaper and hang your coat over here. Don't worry about a little water. You think with seven kids coming home from school this afternoon the house stayed dry?"

Mal led me into her cheerful, slightly chaotic house. I like to visit the Pikes, but it would make me crazy to live here. I knew, though, that her home and family were what Mal missed most when she was away at school.

Claire, who's five, ran ahead of Mal and me into the kitchen, where her sisters — Margo (seven) and Vanessa (nine) — were having a snack.

"Where are the boys?" I asked.

Mal pointed her thumb downstairs. "Rec room," she said. "Not sure what they're doing, but they're quiet."

I made a face. Quiet isn't necessarily a good thing. The Pike boys — eight-year-old Nicky and the ten-year-old triplets, Byron, Adam, and Jordan — can get into an awful lot of trouble whether they're being noisy or quiet. But when I peeked at them I saw that they were reading comic books.

When the girls finished their snacks they joined the boys and their stack of comics. Not ten minutes later I heard Claire say, "I'm bored." This didn't worry me until I heard Nicky and Adam say the same thing.

"Okay." I jumped to my feet and peered outside. Still raining. Uh-oh. "How about a game of Clue?" I suggested.

"No, that's too hard for me," said Claire.

"How about making — "

Jordan cut Mal off before she could even finish her sentence. "No crafts," he said firmly.

I'm not sure now why I did this, but for some reason I found myself telling the kids about the letters my classmates and I were writing.

Claire looked puzzled. "But what kinds of things are you telling yourself?" she wanted to know.

"Things I'll want to read about in four years."

"Are you writing about things you're doing now?" said Byron. "Things that are happening now?"

"Those are the kinds of things you would put in a time capsule," spoke up Vanessa.

"What's a time capsule?" asked Margo.

"A time capsule is . . ." I looked helplessly at Mal. How do you describe a time capsule?

Mal spoke thoughtfully. "When people make a time capsule," she began, "they collect things that are representative of a place or time — things that show what it is like — and they put them in a box or something and then bury the box. Sometime in the future the box is opened, and the people who look at the things inside feel like they're looking into the past."

"What do you mean, things that show what something is like?" asked Nicky.

"Well, if we were making a Pike time capsule we might put one of Vanessa's poems in it, since she writes so much poetry," said Mal. "Or we could put in a photo of our house or a report card one of you guys brings home — anything that's about us right now. Then when we looked at the things in the future they would show us what the past was like."

"Cool," said Byron.

"Let's do it! Let's make a Pike time capsule," said Vanessa. She was practically quivering with excitement.

"Yeah!" cried the other kids.

"How do we start?" asked Margo.

"Let's start by making a list of things we could put in it," said Mal.

So Mal got out a pad of paper and a pen, and her brothers and sisters began tossing out ideas. But my thoughts had gone off in a different direction. Suddenly I had a great plan, almost Kristy-like in its brilliance. I couldn't wait until our BSC meeting that afternoon to tell everyone about it.

❋ Kristy

June 5

Great BSC meeting this afternoon. MA had fabulous idea. Everyone behind it. Just like old days when we used to do this all the time. LOVE having big project to involve kids in. Timing isn't great for us sitters in terms of finals, but kids can work independently on this after we explain it to them.

Only wish had thought of it myself.

Note to self: Think up lots and lots of projects for the

kids this summer. Then BSC will be so caught up in them that we won't be able to slow club down, even in fall when going to that other school.

At exactly 5:27, Stacey and Claud and I heard thundering on the Kishis' stairs, and a moment later Mary Anne rushed into Claud's bedroom, followed by Mallory.

"Mal!" Stacey exclaimed.

"I thought I'd come to the meeting, since Mary Anne was on her way here after she left my house. I hope you don't mind, Kristy."

"No, this is *great*," I said, missing the days when seven or eight of us used to be crowded into the room.

"Plus, I got an idea this afternoon, and Mal can help me explain it," said Mary Anne.

"Cool. What's your idea?" asked Claud.

"Ahem," I said.

"Oh, sorry. Go ahead, Kristy." Claud settled herself on the bed and gave me her full attention.

"Thank you. Okay. This meeting of the Baby-sitters Club will now come to order. Any new business?"

36

Mal's hand shot in the air. "I have news!"

"My idea?" said Mary Anne, looking wounded.

"No. I wouldn't tell them your idea. I have news about Jessi. I didn't say anything this afternoon," Mal went on, glancing at Mary Anne, "because I was hoping I could tell everyone at once. At the meeting."

"But wait. Any actual club business?" I asked. "Schedule changes? Problems?" No one spoke. "Okay. Mal? Your news. And then you can tell us your idea, Mary Anne."

"My news," Mal began, sounding important, "is that Jessi and a couple of other students at her dance school have been selected to join a dance company that is going to go on a world tour this summer. Can you imagine? A *world tour*. They're going to go to *eight* countries." (Jessi, who's a sixth-grader like Mal, is an extremely talented ballet dancer. She studies at a special school in Stamford and has already appeared in lots of productions. In fact, the reason she dropped out of the BSC was because she had been accepted into an intensive program at the dance school.)

"Oh. My. God," said Stacey. "This is so cool."

"What an opportunity," I said.

And then we all began talking at once. When we

settled down, I turned to Mary Anne. "Okay. Now tell us about your idea."

"Well," said Mary Anne, "Mal and I were sitting at her house this afternoon, as you know, and the kids were bored because they were cooped up inside, so I told them about the letters we're writing to ourselves, and somehow we started talking about time capsules — "

"And now my brothers and sisters want to make a Pike time capsule." Mal couldn't help interrupting.

"So they started planning that," Mary Anne went on, "but I thought — why not make a bigger time capsule? One that all our sitting charges could contribute to? A time capsule for our neighborhood in Stoneybrook."

"Oh! What a cool idea!" I cried. "Let's see. We should plan a meeting for all the kids who want to be involved."

"Yeah. We'll have to explain to them what a time capsule *is*," said Mary Anne.

"My brothers and sisters didn't quite understand at first," Mal added.

"Okay. That's easy," I said. "All right. Let me think. The things they put in the capsule could be about the world today, or about Stoneybrook, or the neighborhood, or even their families. Anything that will make a picture of our neighborhood right now."

"They should probably write up explanations of the things they contribute to the capsule," Claudia spoke up.

"That would be helpful," said Stacey.

"Where will we bury the capsule?" asked Mal.

We thought for a few minutes and finally decided on Mary Anne's yard, which is big and also a central place.

"And when will the capsule be dug up?" Stacey wondered.

That was a fascinating thought — digging up our capsule sometime in the future. We talked and talked. Did we want to open the capsule in a hundred years? In five years?

"In seven years," I said slowly, "the oldest kids we sit for now — the triplets and other ten-year-olds — will be going off to college. It might be fun to open the capsule that summer. Before they go away."

"That is so weird," said Mal. "In seven years the triplets will be going to *college*. And I will have been *in* college for a year already."

"We'll be going into our *senior* year in college," said Mary Anne.

"Oh, I can't think about it!" I cried.

But we talked about it anyway, of course. Then we decided where and when to hold the meeting with the kids.

I was grateful to think about the meeting instead of the future.

❀ Claudia

From: ckishi
Subject: grate idea
To: NYCGirl
Date: Monday, June 5
Time: 8:14:44 P.M.

This is a day of grate ideas. Mary ann had one this aftrenoon and know I have one its a REALY grate idea. I cant wait to tell you about it but I am gong to wait anyway. I'll tell you at lunch to-morow when I can tell Kristy and Maryanne and Abby too. Are you exited? It really is a good idea.

   Ok now I am going back to my studying. I am geting VERY nervouse about the math finale.

Love Claud

I was so excited about my idea that, at least for the rest of the evening, it even drove away some of my thoughts about flunking my final exams. But the moment I walked into the school the next morning, those awful thoughts came flooding back. Everywhere were signs that we eighth-graders were about to graduate. And each one reminded me that *I* might *not* graduate.

The first thing Stacey and I saw when we entered SMS was a notice about where and when to pick up our caps and gowns.

"Cool!" cried Stacey. "Imagine us in our caps and gowns, Claud. Our parents are going to take thousands of pictures of us."

"Not if we're not wearing them," I replied.

"What?"

"I have to pass my exams first," I pointed out.

"Oh, you'll pass," said Stacey breezily.

"I have flunked many things in my life."

"That doesn't mean you aren't a wonderful and talented person."

"Thank you. I appreciate that." (Coming from Stacey so soon after our fight, I especially appreciated it.) "But it doesn't make me a better student. Remember my science midterm last year? Remember my math midterm this year? Remember when I was in seventh grade and you were in eighth?"

Suddenly Stacey looked worried. "What do you think will happen if you flunk your exams?"

"Well, I don't think I'm going to flunk *all* of them."

"All right. What do you think will happen if you flunk one of them? Math, for instance?"

"That's the one I'm worried about. And . . . I don't know what will happen. I'm afraid to ask. I think I better just hope I pass everything."

"I'll help you study," Stacey offered. "I can give you special help with math."

"Thank you." I smiled at her. "I accept."

"Excellent. Now, what's your idea about?"

"I'm not telling. Not until lunch."

"Please? Won't you puh-*lease* just give me a little clue?"

"Nope. I want to surprise everyone at once."

"Hey, look." Stacey was pointing to a banner outside the library. Huge red letters said, CONGRAT-ULATIONS, SMS 8TH-GRADERS! A bulletin posted at the end of the sign read, *In order to graduate, all students must return overdue library books by June 20.*

"Well, that's one thing that won't keep me from graduating," I said. "I don't have any overdue library books."

The first bell rang then, and Stacey and I hurried to our lockers.

"See you," I called.

"Later," replied Stacey.

By lunchtime I was starving. But instead of heading for the food line, I ran for our table. Kristy was already sitting at it, opening her bag lunch.

"Where's everyone else?" I asked.

"In line," she replied.

"In *line*? But I can't wait that long to tell them my idea."

"Chill, Claud. Why don't you get in line too? You can tell us while we're eating."

"Oh no, oh no. I can't wait any longer. I really can't." I was like a little kid on Christmas morning who has been told she can't open any presents until after her parents have had their coffee.

"Claudia." Kristy looked sternly at me.

"Okay, okay."

Ten minutes later, Abby, Kristy, Mary Anne, Stacey, and I were seated around our table.

"Don't make me wait another second!" I cried. "I have to tell you my idea now."

"What idea?" said Abby, taking a huge bite of a sandwich.

"My idea! My idea! I had a great idea and I was waiting until we were together at lunch to tell you. So now I'm telling you. And I already asked my parents about this and they said it's okay. I'm going to have a party for us after graduation."

"Oh, excellent! A party just for us?" said Stacey.

"Well, for the Baby-sitters Club members. So for Jessi and Mal too. And Dawn, if she'll be here by then. Will she be here, Mary Anne?"

"Yup. She's going to be at graduation."

"So we'll go to my house after graduation. And we'll have a party in my room."

"Just like an old Baby-sitters Club meeting," said Kristy.

"Exactly," I replied.

"We can remember all the good times we've had together at SMS," said Mary Anne, and I thought her eyes looked a bit teary.

"And all the good times we've had baby-sitting," added Kristy.

"Yeah. Which will be important because I'm not

sure I'm going to be able to do much sitting this summer," said Stacey. "I want to go into New York to be with Dad and Samantha pretty often — like maybe every weekend — and in between I'll want to help out with Mom's store."

"I want to help out too," I said to Stacey. "The store is going to be so cool."

"Are you going to have any time for sitting?" Kristy asked me.

I cleared my throat. "Well . . ."

While I was struggling for an answer, Mary Anne said, "Actually, Dawn and I were thinking of taking a little time off this summer. You know, not working at all, because once ninth grade starts we're going to be awfully busy."

I glanced at Kristy then. She was staring hard at the table.

"Well, that's why the party is going to be sooooo good," I said brightly.

❋ Stacey

From: NYCGirl
Subject: Back to the Future
To: MRDALI
Date: Wednesday, June 7
Time: 7:59:10 P.M.

Dear Ethan,
   Hi! How's everything going? How's the final project for sculpture coming along?
   I've been studying a LOT for finals and also have started to help Claud study for her math final. But this afternoon I took a break and we had a really fun time with a bunch of the kids we sit for. Mary Anne had this great idea to help them make a time capsule, so we met with

the kids this afternoon to tell them about the project. Much excitement.

The plans for Mom's store are really coming along. I like that Mom is letting me help her so much. I feel almost like a partner.

Okay. Back to my French review. Write when you have time.

Love, Stace

The kids who wanted to help make the time capsule gathered in Mary Anne's yard this afternoon. We had phoned lots of our sitting charges the day before to tell them about the meeting, and today twenty-two kids showed up. (Kristy was thrilled.) Thank goodness all four regular BSC members plus Mal were there.

When I arrived at Mary Anne's house, she and Claudia were waiting in the yard, and Kristy was just arriving, with Karen and Andrew in tow. A few minutes later Mal showed up with every single one of her brothers and sisters. Then Mrs. Newton walked Jamie into the yard, followed by Charlotte Johanssen and Haley and Matt Braddock. Fifteen minutes later the three Rodowsky boys, Marilyn and Carolyn Arnold, and the Kuhn kids arrived as well.

"Wow," said Kristy as she counted heads.

We waited five more minutes to see whether anyone else would appear, and then Kristy stood up on an old milk carton and blew a whistle that was hanging around her neck.

"Attention!" she cried, and the kids quieted down. "Okay, we are here to tell you about an exciting idea. How many of you know what a time capsule is?"

Quite a few hands shot in the air, including all of the Pike kids'.

"We made one in our classroom," Jake Kuhn called out.

"Do you want to explain what you did?" Kristy asked him.

"Okay." Jake paused to think. "First we took a big tin box — "

"Like this one?" Kristy interrupted him.

Jake looked at the enormous tin can she was holding up. Mary Anne had just given it to Kristy. Someone had sent it to her when her family had moved into their new house. It had been filled with three gallons of popcorn.

"Yeah, kind of like that. And we filled it with things about our school. We put in one of our lunch menus, and a program from an assembly, and some of the work we've done to show what we've been studying, and a school newspaper article about a field trip we took. Stuff like that. Then we buried it on the playground. Our teacher said that sometime way in the future some other kids will dig it up and open it and they can find out what our school was like in the past."

"Excellent," said Kristy, sounding like a teacher. "And that's pretty much what we thought we'd do. Except our time capsule is going to be about *us*. The way we are right now. So the things we'll put in our time capsule can be about ourselves or our neighborhood or even the world — as long as they make a picture of us now. Do you understand?"

The kids nodded and murmured, and a few hands were raised.

"Is that going to be our time capsule?" asked Haley, pointing to the popcorn tin.

"Yes," replied Kristy, "so keep that in mind when you're deciding what to put in the capsule. Nothing too big, okay?"

"When are we going to bury the time capsule?" asked Nicky Pike.

"Two weeks from today."

Two weeks from today was two days before our graduation. I felt butterflies in my stomach at the very thought.

50

"So come back here to Mary Anne's house then," Kristy went on, "and we'll put your things in the capsule and bury it in the yard."

"How long will it stay buried?" wondered Carolyn Arnold.

"That's a good question. We thought you guys could open it in seven years. That will be right before the oldest of you will be going off to college."

I heard a choking sound from the direction of the triplets.

"College?" croaked Byron.

"Seven years? In seven years I'll be . . . I'll be *fifteen*," cried Charlotte. "In high school. Older than you are now," she said to me.

"And I'll be fourteen," said Karen Brewer. "Older than you, Kristy!"

"I'll be six . . . seven . . . eight . . . nine . . . How old will I be?" Claire asked Mallory.

"You'll be twelve."

Claire looked as if she might faint.

The kids became distracted by imagining themselves seven years in the future, and Kristy eventually had to blow her whistle to recapture their attention. Twenty minutes later the meeting ended, and everyone left, their minds filled with thoughts of the present and of the future.

❋ Mary Anne

Why, you may wonder, is this note wrapped around a piece of burned wood? I know it's a funny thing to put in a time capsule, but this little chunk of wood represents lots of important things to me.

I am Mary Anne Spier, and as I write this I am thirteen years old. I have lived in Stoneybrook all my life. In fact, I live in the house on the property where the time capsule will be buried. By the time the capsule is opened, I'll be twenty years old and in college.

I didn't always live in this house. I was born over on Bradford Court and I lived there until my dad met my stepmom. When they got married we moved to an old, old house with a barn. I loved that house. But it burned down not long ago. And when it burned, everything we owned burned too. But not our memories.

The fire was a tragedy, of course, but some good things did come from it. I learned that memories can't be destroyed. I may not have books or photos anymore, but I still have all my memories of the house and my family and my past. No one and nothing can take them from me. Also, I saw (and not for the first time) how wonderful our neighbors are. The night of the fire people came by with clothing and all sorts of offers of help. Friends took us in to stay with them. Later, neighbors helped us find a place to stay while we decided what we were going to do. And eventually we decided to convert the barn into a brand-new house. It's that new house you're looking at while you open the time capsule.

The old house, the one that burned, represented lots of things to me. One of them was a chunk of the time I spent with my friends in the Baby-sitters Club. And if it weren't for the BSC (which, I have a feeling, no longer exists), there wouldn't be any time capsule. Kristy Thomas, the president of the BSC, has been really important to the kids in this neighborhood. She was the one who organized us to make this time capsule (although I have to admit that the neighborhood time capsule itself was MY idea).

When the house burned, my life changed. The fire set me on a path to a new life. That was

both good and bad.
I don't regret the fire,
though. Mostly. I
am so happy that
after the fire my family
decided to stay right
here in our neighborhood
in Stoneybrook. I can't
think of a better place
in which to grow up.

❀ Mallory

Name: Mallory Pike

Age: 11

As you can see, I am putting a pamphlet from the Stoneybrook Chamber of Commerce in this time capsule. (Note to whomever is reading this: I hope the pamphlet is still attached to this letter.) I'm sure that seven years from now, when you are looking through our time capsule, Stoneybrook will be a different place. But not too different. Anyway, this pamphlet will show you which stores and restaurants were here in this year, and will tell you the population of Stoneybrook and other current facts and figures.

Things I like about Stoneybrook: It's on the water. It's in New England. It's near Stamford, a biggish city, and not too far from NYC, but it is definitely a small town. Most people here are very friendly. There are lots of things for kids to do.

Things I don't like about Stoneybrook: It's so small that sometimes it feels suffocating. Some people here are definitely not friendly and need to work on their attitudes.

I feel a little funny writing about Stoneybrook and our neighborhood. That's because this year I went away to a private school in Massachusetts. So I don't feel as much a part of Stoneybrook as I once did. And I have to say that when I first went away I couldn't wait to get out of here. I was having trouble at SMS, and I was really uncomfortable there. I didn't fit in with the kids. Going off to school every day was torture! Then I was accepted at this special arts school, and suddenly school is great again.

I'll tell you who I feel like: Dorothy Gale, from *The Wizard of Oz*. Like Dorothy, I left my home hurt and angry and went off to a new and wonderful place. But now that I've been away for a while, I think I appreciate Stoneybrook more. It will always be a part of me. I was born here and I lived here for eleven years. And when I talk about "home" I mean Stoneybrook. I have a feeling I always will, no matter where I live.

❀ Kristy

Dear Kristy,
So how are you, four years later?
I am fine.

Dear Kristy,
You are seventeen when you are
reading this

Dear Kristy,
I am thirteen now

Dear you

Dear Kristy,
It is the very end of eighth grade.
In a week and a half I will
graduate and leave sms behind

forever. Mr. Kingbridge told us to write about all this personally meaningful stuff — defining events and so forth.

Well, I guess the defining event of my life was when my father walked out on our family. That was seven years ago (when I was six), and it changed everything. Absolutely everything. Dad left us with almost no money, and Mom had to work hard to support Charlie and Sam and David Michael and me. She barely earned enough money to pay for food and stuff, so how was she supposed to pay for child care too? It was very hard for a long time. And everyone was and still is really mad at my father. You would think the least he could do after leaving like that would be to call every now and then. But no

I stopped writing. Was this what I wanted to read four years from now? I didn't think so. I hardly wanted to read it now. It sounded so bitter.

I decided to try a different approach.

Dear Kristy,

Hi! It's me, Kristy. Well, you know that, of course.

Let me see. La, la-la, la-la. Okeydokey. A defining event in my life was the day I thought up the idea for the Baby-sitters Club. The club has been just great. It has led to all sorts of wonderful, wonderful things, such as friend-ship and money. I am so proud of myself. And of my friends. We really made a success of our business.

"Kristy! Kristy? Are you home? Is anybody home?"

With a huge sigh of relief I put down my pen, ran to the door of my room, and threw it open. "Charlie? Is that you?"

"Yeah. Where is everybody?"

"Well, Mom is at work, of course, and Nannie took the kids downtown. Sam is still at school, I think, but Watson should be in his office. Didn't he hear you?"

Charlie had come pounding up the stairs and had thrown himself across my bed. He was holding a letter. "Maybe Watson's on the phone," he said breathlessly. "I won't disturb him. But Kristy, you have to hear this news!"

"What?" I looked warily at the letter in his hand.

"It's from Boiceville State. I got in! Even though I applied late and everything."

Of course Charlie had gotten in. His grades are excellent. Any school would want him.

I plastered a smile across my face. "Wow! Cool. So you're going to college after all. At least it's nearby. You can still live at home — "

Charlie held up his hand. "Oh, no. That's the best part. I'm going to live on campus. They have room for me. The dorm — "

"But you'll only be forty-five minutes away. Why aren't you going to stay here?"

"Living away from home is half the college experience," said Charlie, sounding as though he were quoting from the college catalog, but also sounding as though he really meant it.

"I guess."

"And you know what else? I think I'm going to apply to UCLA for next year. I don't know what got into me — why I put off applying — because I really want to go to college, and a good one at that."

"UCLA?" I repeated. "Isn't that in California?"

"Yup."

"So you'd be near Dad."

Charlie frowned. "*That* is *not* a *factor*," he said crisply, and I believed him. After an uncomfortable pause he brightened and went on, "UCLA has everything I want. I wonder if I could even transfer midyear, as a freshman. Maybe . . . Well, first I just have to get ready for Boiceville. I have to do really well there, make top grades and all. I have to tell Watson," he went on in a rush. "I don't care if he's on the phone."

Charlie bolted from the room. I looked at my pathetic attempt at a letter to myself. I crumpled the pages and threw them across the room, making three baskets in a row. I did not impress myself. I leaned back against my pillows and put my arm over my eyes.

A week and a half until graduation. Mine. Charlie's.

I didn't want any of it to happen.

I didn't want time to march on. I wanted it to march backward.

❀ Jackie

Here is a softball.
Mom said to tell why I chose the softball for this time capsool. I chose it because it is improtant. It makes me think of Kristy.

Kristy Thomas is good and important. She is improtant to all the kids in Stoneybrok. Kristy likes kids and you can tell. She started Kristy's Krushers. (That word is suposed to be spelled wrong.) The Krushers is a softbell team. It is for all us kids so we can play on a real team with unaforms which are t-shirts and hats.

64

Here are some of the things Kristy does with the Krushers.
1. She practices throwing with us.
2. She practises pithing with us.
3. She shows us things.
4. She spends time with us.
5. She ~~incoo inboo encoo~~ tells us we are doing a good job.
Sometimes we win, sometimes we lose. But with Kristy around we always have fun.
Kristy is kind of like a grownup but kind of like a kid too. She orgenizes softbill games and other things for us kids so we will have fun ~~abte acte~~ projicts.
Whenever I see Kristy coming, I yell inside my head, Look out !!!! Here comes fun !!!!!
Kristy started this thing called the baby-sitters Club. It is really important to us kids here in Stoneybroke.

By Jackie Rodowsky, age 7

P. S.   When you open this capsool,
what are you going to do with
the things inside it? Maybe
I could have this ball back.
It is my best one. I will miss it.
My address is: 6 Reilly Lane
                    Stoneybrook, C.T.
P. P. S. In 7 years I will be 14.
P. P. P. S. Hey maybe I will
 be one of the people opening
 the capsool. Then I can take
 my ball bake myself.

Hello, everybody. The person writing this is Jessica Ramsey, but people call me Jessi. I'm eleven years old now, and I'll be eighteen when this time capsule is opened. I might not be around for the opening. I think I'll be away at college, and busy dancing too.

I have chosen this newspaper article for our time capsule.

*** Read the article now, then come back to my letter ***

Okay. Did you read it? I know. It is not a pleasant article. You are probably wondering why I chose to include an article about racial intolerance in the capsule. Did you notice that the incident described in the article took place right over in Westmoore? That's only nine miles from here. It is a sad fact, but racial intolerance is alive and well in the good old USA at the time I am writing this. In fact, so is intolerance in general. People are intolerant of other people's religious beliefs, nationality, sexual orientation, and physical and mental disabilities. To name a few things. Not very nice, is it?

Guess what. When I first moved to Stoneybrook my family and I met a few people who definitely did not like us because of the color of our skin. They believed that African - Americans did not belong in their neighborhoods, their schools, walking down their streets. This was pretty silly, considering we were not the first African - American family in Stoneybrook.

Things have changed since then. My family and I have been very happy in Stoneybrook and in our neighborhood. But every now and then I read an article like this one and I am reminded that our country has made lots of strides in the last century, but that we still have a long way to go. No person should have to feel afraid or ashamed because of his skin color, because of the religion he practices, because he doesn't speak English, or because he wasn't born in America.

I have been given a great opportunity this summer. I will be touring with a dance company, and I am going to be able to visit other countries, see other people, learn about other cultures. Maybe more people should have the chance to see that all people are created equal, but also that all people are created different.

I hope by the time you are opening this capsule and reading my letter that intolerance will be a thing of the past.

Here are four important words to remember:

Tolerate
Understand
Accept
Embrace

❋ Stacey

Dear Stacey,
   Boy, does that feel weird

   Wait. I can't write that in a letter to myself. Do over.

Dear Stacey,
   A defining event in my life was when I was diagnosed with diabetes. The thing is, even though it was a defining event, I don't want to be defined by it. Does that make sense? There's so much more to me.

   Stop. Why am I telling myself this? I know I have diabetes. And I'll still have it four years from now when I read this letter. Hmm. I see what Kristy meant when she said that writing her letter was a lot harder than she had thought it was going to be.

Dear Stacey,
   It is almost the end of eighth grade, almost time for graduation. I think that two of the things that define me, at least right now, are the fact that I live with diabetes every day, and the fact that my parents are divorced. I know that lots of kids have divorced parents, but it has put a different spin on my life. Like, now I divide my time between my mom and my life in Stoney-brook, and my dad and my life in New York City. My life in New York City now includes Samantha, Dad's fiancée. (Is that spelled right?) I'm not sure when they're going to get married, but it is going to happen and then my family will change again.

I stopped writing. Thinking about Samantha had caused an image of graduation to pop into my head. This was the image: I am standing with my friends behind the podium that will be set up on the grounds of SMS (assuming we have good weather on graduation day), and looking out at the audience — all the gathered friends and family members. In the front row I see Mom, Dad . . . and Samantha. Only not seated in that order. Samantha is *between* Mom and Dad, for some reason. And I can feel the tension from where I am standing. Mom, who has been seething ever since Samantha sat down, pokes Samantha in the side. Samantha pokes her back. Dad pretends not to see this. Then Mom subtly pulls a strand of Samantha's hair, and Samantha yanks a whole handful of Mom's hair. In a flash, a huge fight has broken out. Everyone knows it's my stupid family having the fight and hundreds of pairs of eyes turn on me. I have disrupted the entire graduation ceremony, and I haven't done a thing.

I shuddered. How bad would graduation actually be? Was Samantha going to come? If she did, where would she and Dad stay?

I shook my head and put down my pen. I needed a break. That was when I realized I had forgotten to bring in the mail when I returned home from school.

Perfect excuse to leave my room and walk outside for a breath of air.

I retrieved our mail and leafed through it as I headed back inside.

Hmm. An envelope addressed to me from Stoneybrook Middle School. Now, what could that be? A reminder about something to do with graduation? Probably. Still, as I opened the envelope a funny feeling crept over me. I felt as if I were in second grade and I'd been sent home with a note from the teacher.

This is to inform you, the letter began, *that* <u>Stacey McGill</u> *has* <u>one</u> *overdue book(s) from the Stoneybrook Middle School library. Please return* <u>Ribsy, by Beverly Cleary</u>, *to the library before* <u>June 20</u>. *Please note that 8th-grade students with outstanding library books cannot graduate.*

The funny feeling changed to a feeling of horror. *What?* What was this? I had an overdue library book and I couldn't graduate until I returned it? And that overdue book was a copy of *Ribsy?* When had I taken *Ribsy* out of our library? I couldn't believe I had ever checked it out. *Ribsy* is a fabulous story (I love Beverly Cleary's books), but it is a tad on the babyish side for someone who is about to enter high school.

I knew I hadn't checked the book out this year. It

must have been something I had checked out in seventh grade. Probably near the beginning of seventh grade. Something I needed to read for comfort when I had first moved to Stoneybrook from New York and hardly knew anyone and just wanted to feel little and secure again.

Where on earth was the book? I didn't remember seeing it in my room in recent history. Worse, between the beginning of seventh grade and now I had moved back to New York again and then returned to Stoneybrook. Had the book survived two moves? I didn't think so.

Oh, lord. Oh, lord. This was just horrible. I wasn't going to graduate, and all because of a copy of *Ribsy*.

Dear Stacey,
   I am thirteen years old, and I am an idiot.
                    Love, Stacey

The only good thing about my not being able to graduate was that now my mother and Samantha wouldn't have a fistfight in front of all of SMS.

✷ Kristy

To Whom It May Concern:

I'm not sure exactly who will be opening this time capsule seven years from now. It should be Byron, Jordan, and Adam Pike, along with other people from the neighborhood. But you never know.

Allow me to introduce myself. My name is Kristin Amanda Thomas. As I write this I am thirteen years old. What I have decided to include in the capsule is the attached flier. It is one of the original fliers announcing the formation of the Baby-sitters Club about two years ago. The reason I have chosen it is because without the BSC, this time capsule probably wouldn't be here.

My friends and I started the BSC at the beginning of seventh grade. Since then we have been baby-sitting for lots of the kids around here and also working on fun projects with them, projects like the time capsule. One of the best things about the BSC, for me, has been that it has made me feel so connected to my neighbors, and it has brought friendship and lots of good times. Also, lots of funny times.

Among other things, the BSC members have helped the kids around here put on a talent show, and make baskets to take to the elderly people living in Stoneybrook Manor. We have helped out with a Little Miss Stoneybrook pageant and a baby parade. We have run a summer play group, organized carnivals, and thrown parties. We have solved mysteries and taken trips. Who can forget such things as the kids' performance of <u>The Three Billy Goats Gruff</u>, or when they put on the <u>BSC Follies</u>? My friends and I have baby-sat, dog-sat, and even goat-sat! These have been two of the best years of my life. Well, to be honest, the Baby-sitters Club IS my life.

I hope that when you are reading this, our neighborhood still feels like a community, because that is so important and wonderful.

Maybe this flier and letter will give some of you an idea — and you'll start your own Baby-sitters Club. Feel free to use the name. And if you want to consult me on anything, just look up Thomas in the phone book. I bet we'll still be listed.

✦ Abby

Hey, everybody! I know this is kind of a funny-looking photo album. That's because I made it myself. (Like you couldn't tell.) Why did I make a photo album to put in the time capsule? Good question. Okay, the thing is, I haven't lived in Stoneybrook for very long. My mom and my sister and I moved here from Long Island less than a year ago. So I wasn't sure what to say about Stoneybrook. I mean, I really like it, but... I guess I just don't know it very well yet. I have gotten to know the people, though, and thats' how I came up with the idea for this album.

I thought that seven years from now, whoever opens the capsule might want to see who the major neighbor-hood players were at the time we were putting the capsule together. The team players, so to speak. All right. Without further ado...

1. This is Kristy Thomas, founder of the Baby-sitters Club, head coach of Kristy's Krushers, person extraordinaire. She's the glue of this neighborhood.

2. Claudia Kishi is the vice-president of the BSC — and artist extraordinaire. Also, a junk food connoisseur. A vital part of the BSC.

3. Voila Mary Anne Spier. She has been with the BSC as its secretary since forever. She's a sensitive soul, and kids love her. So do animals.

4. The BSC's valued treasurer is Stacey McGill, formerly of the Big Apple. Stacey can crunch numbers in an annoyingly speedy manner.

5. , Abby Stevenson. C'est moi! A former BSC member and a fledgling Stoneybrookite. I help Kristy with the Krushers sometimes.

6. And this is Jessi Ramsey, dancer extraordinaire and another former BSC member. I'm certain we'll see Jessi's name in lights one day.

7. Here's the Pike family. That one in the middle with the arrow pointing to her is Mallory, yet another former BSC member. Some of our more memorable sitting jobs have taken place at Mal's house with her younger brothers and sisters.

8. Okay, group-shot time. Thanks for posing, you guys. Here are twenty-four of our regular sitting charges. (Look at my handy chart to see who's who.)

9. Here are the Krushers at practice. That's

Jackie Rodowsky at bat. Look out! Don't stand too close! (Jackie is one of our more enthusiastic players.)

10. This is a shot of Bradford Court, where at one time Kristy, Claudia, and Mary Anne all lived. That house on the left is Claudia's, where all BSC meetings are held.

11. Claudia is ready to kill me for this, but here is her bedroom. (Nice underwear, Claud!) That's the phone that job calls come in on. Oh, and that director's chair is where Kristy sits during every meeting.

So that's a little tour of my Stoneybrook and BSC territory. I hope it brings back memories and maybe answers a few questions when you open the time capsule.

Respectfully submitted by,
Abby Stevenson

❀ Claudia

Dear Claudia
How are you. I am fine.

Dear Claud :
Hi its me you. I mean its me —
yourself. But you know that

Dear Claudia
Well your seventeen now. How does
that feel.

I threw my paper down in disgust. What was it
about this letter? It was the hardest thing in the
world to write. Maybe I should just scrap it. There
was no real reason for me to write it. It wasn't an
assignment. I wasn't going to get graded on it. It

wouldn't have any effect on whether I passed and went on to SHS.

But I didn't want to be the only one of my friends who *didn't* write a letter, who *didn't* have an envelope to open at the end of my high school years. Everyone (and by "everyone," I mean Kristy) would be saying, "Did you get your letter, Claud? Did it come yet?"

And I would have to say no.

Which I didn't want to do.

Hmm. I could just mail myself a blank piece of paper or even an empty envelope. Who would know? We were supposed to give Mr. Kingbridge our envelopes all sealed up. The only way to know I had mailed myself a blank piece of paper would be if someone opened the letter before I did, and I believe that is called mail fraud, which is a federal offense.

But how humiliating. When I opened the letter in four years and saw the lame way out I had taken I would be SO embarrassed. It would be a horrible reminder of what a pathetic student I can be.

And speaking of being a pathetic student . . . I looked at the growing stack of papers, books, and notebooks I should have been going through in order to finish studying for my finals. An uneasy feeling crept over me, and I remembered the papers that had been handed back to my classmates and me in science earlier in the day. During this last quarter of the year each of us had had to write a paper on a topic of our choice. The paper was worth twenty-five percent of our final grade. My topic had been "Plants: Can They Really Hear Music?" I had actually performed an experiment, one that had driven certain members of my family nearly crazy. I had grown bean plants in three separate jars. One jar of beans had been placed next to a radio that played nothing but the local classical music station. Another had heard only rock music, and the third had heard no music at all. I had written up my experiment very officially, describing everything, including how the plants looked each day. I had been certain to use professional experimental terms, such as control group (that was for the beans that heard no music at all). The result? All the beans grew pretty much the same way. I decided music didn't have any effect on plants.

I had been proud of my experiment, but I had felt . . . uncertain . . . when I had handed in my paper. Which was why I hadn't looked at it yet to find out my grade. I decided to do that now. I opened my science notebook and pulled out the folder in which I had handed in my paper. I had drawn a lovely portrait of the three jars of beans on the front of the folder, which I had hoped might add a little something to the project in case anything was lacking.

Now, very slowly, I opened the folder. Written at the top of the first page in red ink was a . . . D+.

For a moment, I just stared at it. This large cold lump was forming in my stomach. I tried to ignore it. I tried to get mad at my teacher. What was the stupid point of giving someone a D *plus*? As if the plus would make the D sound any better. Give me a break. A D is a D.

And I was now seriously close to failing science.

I panicked. What should I do? I didn't want to tell my parents what was going on. I had already been in so much trouble. And what if they decided that the best thing for me to do was to repeat eighth grade? I just couldn't let that happen. My friends absolutely could not go on to high school without me. That would be way more humiliating than when I had to repeat seventh grade.

I grabbed the phone and dialed Stacey's number. She answered on the first ring.

"Stacey, it's me, and I'm in terrible trouble," I said in a rush.

"What? What is it? Where are you? Are you hurt?"

"Not that kind of trouble," I replied. "But I really think I'm going to flunk science."

"Claud, do *not* call a person and say you are in terrible trouble unless you mean — "

"I won't, I won't." I didn't even let her finish speaking. "I'm sorry. But listen, this is really serious." I explained what had happened. "What am I going to do?"

Stacey thought for a moment. "I'll tutor you in science too," she said finally. "I'm not as good in science as I am in math, but I'm doing fine, so I think I can help you. We'll just buckle down and start working, okay?"

"Really? Oh, Stacey, that would be great. I don't know how to thank you. I — "

"I'll be right over," Stacey interrupted me.

I sighed. Just like the old days.

I turned back to my books and felt a teeny bit better.

✳ Stacey

By Anastasia Elizabeth McGill

Hello to all you people of the future. My name is Stacey McGill, and I moved to Stoneybrook when I was twelve years old. Until then I had lived in New York City. I love Stoneybrook. In fact, when my parents got divorced, I was given the choice of living with my dad in New York or with my mom here. I chose here. It was a really difficult decision, of course, since I love both of my parents, and since I had grown up in NYC. But the truth is, I'd already felt that Stoneybrook was my home. Why? The piece of paper I have attached to this one should help explain.

Take a look at the heading on the paper:
STARS OF TOMORROW
Talent Show

I don't know if anyone opening this time capsule will remember that show, but I sure do. It took place in the Pikes' backyard, and half the neighborhood was in the show. (The rest of the neighborhood turned out to watch it.) As you can see from the list of acts that Vanessa announced to the audience, Sean Addison played his tuba, Buddy Barrett showed off Pow the basset hound's tricks, and Nicky Pike performed on stilts to "Yankee Doodle Dandy." Those were just some of the acts. I remember that the Pike triplets built a stage for the event and sold tickets to the show at the entrance to their yard. It was quite a day.

Why have I included this in the time capsule? Because it is just so . . . Stoneybrook. Things like this go on in our neighborhood all the time. Maybe that doesn't mean much to most people, but it does to me. When I was growing up, I lived in a high-rise apartment building. I had a few friends in the building, of course, and I knew some of the people who lived and worked on our block. I guess the block was my neighborhood. But nothing like the talent show ever happened there.

This neighborhood, our community here in Stoneybrook, is very special, at least to me. The people here have become some of my closest friends, and I know that when I'm grown up I'll find happy memories when I look back on this time. I hope that seven years from now Stoneybrook won't have changed much, and that the kids who open the time capsule will be creating their own happy memories.

❀ Claire

Claire Pike, age 5
As dictated to Vanessa Pike, age 9

Hello, my name is Claire Pike.
I live on Slate Street in Stoneybrook, CT. This is what I am
putting in the time capsule — my
bear, Ba-ba. (Don't worry,
Kristy, Ba-ba is a very small
bear. She won't take up too
much room in the tin box.)
Why I chose Ba-ba is
because she is my favorite
bear and she is very important
to me. I got Ba-ba when I
was born. I mean, someone
gave her to me. I think it

was my uncle Joe who is really my great-uncle. But I guess it doesn't matter who gave her to me. It just matters that she is a special bear. Ba-ba has been with me every single day of my life. I sleep with her at night. Ba-ba has come on all our vacations. I even make presents for her. Ba-ba's birthday is the same as mine, and I always make her a card or something, and on Christmas I make her a little hat or her own book, and last Christmas I gave her my old tea set, which she really likes. Everyone in my family waits to see what I will give Ba-ba. Nobody else gives her presents. But nobody else loves Ba-ba the way I do.

I know Ba-ba doesn't look very pretty anymore. I have seen pictures of her when she was new, and she was much fluffier and cleaner then, and she had two ears and two eyes that matched. Now her fur is kind of matted down and one ear got torn off by Pow, and also one of her eyes is the glass one she came with, but the other is just a brown button Mallory sewed on when the second glass one came off. Still, she is my Ba-ba and I love her.

And that is why I think she belongs in the time capsule.

Love,
Claire Pike

* * * SPECIAL NOTE * * *

It's me, Vanessa Pike, writing now. Claire doesn't know I am adding this to her note. I just want to say that obviously Claire doesn't understand what a time capsule really is, or she wouldn't have chosen Ba-ba to put in it. I think Claire thinks the capsule is more of a keepsake box. I tried to explain that the things the kids are putting in the capsule should be about Stoneybrook or our neighborhood, but Claire kept saying that Ba-ba is the most important thing she can think of. I asked Mallory what to do about this and she said just go ahead and let Claire participate in her own way. And that is why Ba-ba is in the time capsule.

— Vanessa Pike

❀ Dawn

Dawn Schafer

Address:
  22 Buena Vista
  Palo City, CA 92800

Summer Address:
  177 Burnt Hill Road
  Stoneybrook, CT 06800

  I guess some of
you are looking at this
and wondering why
someone who lives in
California has been
asked to participate

in the Stoneybrook
time capsule project.
Well, the truth is, even
though I was born
and raised in California,
I've also been a Stoney-
brookite. I lived here
for a memorable time
in my life. While I was
in Stoneybrook, I made
a group of fabulous
friends, AND my mom
got remarried and I
acquired the world's
best stepsister and also
a pretty nice stepfather.
This means that I now
have two families, which
I think makes me
lucky. The only unlucky
thing about the arran-
gement is that my
families live on opposite
coasts. Still, I get to
spend summers and
vacations in Stoneybrook,
and live in California
the rest of the time.

Anyway, I have chosen to put these pages from _The Stoney-brook News_ in the time capsule. I know they're just a bunch of ads, but I think they'll be interesting a few years from now. Look at the airfares in the ads for the travel agencies. If anyone knows about airfares, it's me (and my parents and step-parents), since my brother, Jeff, and I fly cross-country several times a year. It's expensive enough now; I wonder what it will cost by the time you open the capsule.

There are other ads on these pages too—for prom gowns from Bellair's, and CDs from Sound Ideas, and earrings from the Merry-Go-Round. I bet these stores will still be around when the capsule is opened. If they are, check out their ads and compare them to these. You'll probably say how cheap everything was when the time capsule was put together. But let me tell you, these things do not seem cheap now!

Well, who knows? In seven years, maybe air travel will have changed somehow and it won't be so expensive. Maybe it'll be even faster too. Maybe I'll be able to zoom back and forth between Palo City and Stoney-brook in just a couple of hours — and pay for it myself out of my allowance. If that happened, I might spend more time in Stoneybrook. It's been a second home to me, but the less time I spend here the less connected I feel to it, and I don't like that. If you live in Stoneybrook now, enjoy it. It's a great place to live!

Yours bicoastally,
Dawn Schafer

❀ Mary Anne

Hello there!

Dear Self,

Dear Mary Anne,

A letter to myself:

Dear Mary Anne,
Today it is
sunny and warm,
a fine June day

Well. Everyone has told me how much trouble they're having with their letters, but for some reason I didn't think I would have trouble with mine. I just assumed that when I sat down with my notebook, the words and thoughts would flow. But it is SO WEIRD to try to write to myself in the future.

What things have been important in my life? The fact that I never knew my mother, that I grew up in the tiny world of Dad and me, that we lost everything in a fire? These things *are* important — I know that — but there's so much more to my life right now.

I guess I think of my life in terms of the people in it. Maybe you could even say that my life is defined by the people in it. I don't know. Mr. Kingbridge told us to talk about defining moments. I think that's what he said, anyway. I'm having trouble remembering his exact words. Well, I do remember that he said to write a letter that I would find meaningful and interesting when I read it in four years. So I suppose I can write whatever I feel like writing about.

Maybe I'll just select several people who are important to me and write a paragraph or two about each of them. This won't be a conventional letter, but so what. Now . . . who should I write about? Or is it "whom" should I write about? Oh, brother. If I get hung up on stuff like that, this letter will not be finished on time. All right. The important people in my life are Dad, Dawn, Sharon, my grandparents, Jeff,

Kristy, Claudia, Jessi, Stacey, Abby, Mal, Kristy's mom, Karen, Andrew . . . Hmm. That's quite a list. And I haven't mentioned people who are no longer alive who have been very important to me — Mom and Mimi.

Then, of course, there's Logan.

Okay, let me focus on the others for the moment.

Kristy. I don't know why I've decided to start with Kristy. She's not a family member, but she is, well, hard to ignore. Kristy and I have known each other since we were babies. When I think of Kristy, I think of a person who has always been a part of my life.

I paused. I put down my pen. I read the paragraph I'd just written about Kristy. It was nice enough, but why was I telling myself about Kristy? I had a strong suspicion that four years from now Kristy and I would still be best friends (I think we always will be), and when I opened my letter I would wonder why I had written about our early years together.

I stood up. I cracked my knuckles. I looked around my brand-new bedroom. I sought inspiration from the scene outside my window, from the wall, from the floor. Nothing came to me. I remembered once when I had been in a session with my therapist and I couldn't find the words to talk about something or other. Finally my therapist told me I was "blocked." That was how I felt now. Blocked. What was preventing me from writing my letter? I didn't even seem able to write a rough draft of it.

My eyes settled on a photo of Logan that was on the bureau. Logan had given me the photo shortly after the fire, when I realized that along with everything else that had been lost, our albums and pictures were gone. Then my mind settled on Logan as well.

In my life, Logan is unfinished business. He should be finished business. When I told him it was time for us to stop seeing each other I meant it. I really meant it. I was tired of Logan and tired of so many things about our relationship. I had thought, *For heaven's sake, Logan and I are only thirteen years old. We shouldn't be so tied to each other. We should see other people. Who could expect us to be together forever?* We'd already broken up once. And I had felt it was time for us to break up again. Permanently. Before we got to high school, so we could be free to go out with other people when we were there.

And yet, now that we weren't speaking, now that Logan did occasionally see other girls, why did my decision seem . . . not quite right? I remembered all the things that had been wrong with our relationship — and suddenly they seemed fixable.

Which was why I headed into Dad and Sharon's room and sat in the armchair next to the telephone table. I picked up the phone. I set it back in the cradle. I picked up the phone again and dialed the first three digits of Logan's number. I set the phone back in the cradle. I picked up the phone once more and dialed five digits before I hung up. Six digits. Then the complete number. When I heard Logan's sister, Kerry, say hello, I hung up again.

With a huge sigh, I returned to my room. I pulled a fresh sheet of paper out of my notebook and wrote, *Dear Logan*. Then I crumpled it up and threw it away. Finally I headed downstairs to start dinner for Dad and Sharon.

I had made a decision.

I needed to talk to Logan.

❁ Claudia

Well, as you can see by this flyer
Stoneybrooks 250th brithday is
coming up this sumer so when you
open this capsole stoneybrok will be
257 years old. All I have heard about
for the last yar or so is the birthday
celabration it is a very big Deal. (one
reason I have heard so much about
it is because my parents are on all
these ~~cori~~ ~~comtea~~ they have been
active in planning the events.

Well I guess when you think about
it 250 yars is a really long time.
One thing I like about Stoneybrook
is that it does have this history. and
I like that the history is important

To the poeple who live here.

Here are some of the things that will be gong on in Stoneybrok this summer

(1.) Special fire works on the 4th of July

(2. A new stateue for the square downtown it will be a carving of general John bradshaw one of the founders of Stoneybrook

3) every store in town will sell tshirts that say Stoneybrook — 250 yars young

4. On the actual brithday of the town there will be a enormus parade with flots and everything. I have been working on several of the flots and with any luck I will get to ride on one to.

5. The kids in Stoneybrok elementry school have been making displays for the window of the public librery. Some of the displays are "Stoneybrook's coastal History" and "mysteries of Stoneybrok" and "Our Roll in the revalutonary war".

6) The Town Players are going to put on a originale play about Stoneybrooks part in the Undergrond Railroad.

There are some other events too (look at the flyer.) It's really exciting!!! And I think it's cool that this time capsole is being buried in the year of our 250th britnday celebraton.

And check this out because I'm really proud of it — I did the artwork on the flyer. Which reminds me to mention that in 7 years I hope to be a famouse artist. Or an almost famouse artist.

Yours Truly,
Claudia Kishi

❀ Charlotte

Charlotte Theresa Johanssen
9 years old

I think one of the
best things about
Stoneybrook is
Stoneybrook Element-
ary school. That's my
school. And that's the
reason I wanted to
put our school news-
paper in the time
capsule. The newspaper
is the thing I clipped
to this paper. It is
called the Stoneybrook
Examiner, even though

I don't think it examines very much.

I thought it would be interesting for whoever opens the time capsule to see what our school used to be like. So take a look at the newspaper. See? On the back page are our lunch menus for June. The pizza burgers are really good. The corn on the cob is not. It is never fresh. But the ice cream is usually good. And so is the apple crisp. We are lucky to have a cafeteria with so much good food in it. (Even the corn is really OK.)

Now, on page 3 are field trips. You can read all about them. Mr. Barnes's class took a field trip to the bakery in Stanford. (Everyone got a free doughnut to eat on the bus going home.) Ms. Casey's class took a trip to the aquarium, and Ms. Dreeben's class took a trip to the Animal Rescue Foundation.

Well, on page 5 is news from the classes, and on page 1 are announcements, and also on page 1 is the schedule of after-school activities. If you are part of the after-school program you can go to Homework Help or Arts and Crafts or Music Appreciation or Softball or Creative Writing (that one is my favorite) or Kids Cooking or sometimes something special like Puppetry.

Now I have to say that if you look at page 6 you will see something I am very proud of. I wrote an essay about someone who is important in my life. I chose my baby-sitter Stacey McGill — and my teacher told me my essay was going to be published in the Examiner! So you can also read about my best grown-up friend in this paper. Stacey is the nicest person in the world. I know you shouldn't really pick favorites, especially since I have so many nice baby-sitters, but I couldn't help it. I call Stacey my almost-sister. And I hope when we open this capsule — when I am 16 and Stacey is 20 —

that we will still be almost-sisters.

And I am sure that in 7 years Stoneybrook Elementary will still be the best school in town. School rules!

❀ Stacey

Okay. I managed to do it. I have finally written the letter to myself, and I think it is okay. No, it's good. I think I'll be pleased and interested when I read it in four years. It paints a pretty accurate picture of my life now, and it includes my thoughts for the future. (They may be fairly entertaining when I read about them later.) Anyway, here is my finished letter:

Dear Stacey,
   **Greetings! This is a voice from the past —
your voice. It is June as I write this, almost the
end of school, which this year means the end of
eighth grade, and graduation from SMS. In the
fall I'll be a freshman at SHS. I'm scared and ner-**

vous, but just a little. Mostly I'm excited. I feel ready for bigger things.

Here are the bare facts about my life right now (to give you something to compare your life to). Mom and Dad have been divorced for awhile and have settled into their lives in Stoneybrook and New York City. Mom has been on a couple of dates, but absolutely none that was serious. I don't think she's in any rush to be in another relationship. She's going to concentrate on her career instead. At the moment she is planning to open her own store, which is so exciting. I hope she really can go ahead with it and that in four years it will be a big success. It will be so cool to see newspaper ads for it and things like that.

Dad is another story. He is still a workaholic, AND he is already in another relationship. In fact, he and Samantha are going to get married soon. Maybe when you read this in four years you'll be a big sister! I know Samantha wants to have children and I bet Dad does too. After all, he had a pretty nice kid the first time around. In four years I would really like to have a little sister and a little brother, one of each.

Currently, my closest friends are Claudia, Mary Anne, and Kristy, the other members of the Baby-sitters Club. I used to feel that Claud was my best friend, but I can't say that anymore. Our fight really changed things. I would do anything for Claud — absolutely — but I don't feel quite the same way about her that I did even a few months ago. And Mary Anne and Kristy are fabulous, but (and maybe this will make you laugh in four years) I suspect that by the time we graduate they may not be my closest friends anymore. I think we'll have other really close friends, friends we'll make in SHS. No doubt about it, though, the BSC (the club itself as well as the people in it) has been one of the most important things in my life the last couple of years. I think I will always look back on it that way.

The most important boy in my life at the moment is Ethan. Four years from now? Hard to predict. I bet we'll still know each other, but will we still see each other as (potential) boyfriend and girlfriend? I just can't say. Ethan will have been in college for a couple of years already, so we'll be in pretty different places in our lives.

Some of the things that I think have helped

me to be the person I am today (the defining events Mr. Kingbridge talked about) are my diabetes, and Mom and Dad's relationship, including the divorce. I see myself as a pretty strong person, and I expect to be even stronger in four years. I think I'm strong because of facing and dealing with these situations. The diabetes has shown me that I can't always be in control, but it has given me a sense of control. I mean, when I was first diagnosed with diabetes I had to understand that sometimes things just happen that we can't control. But then I learned how to follow a diet and regulate my insulin, and that gave me back a feeling of control — one that I don't take for granted.

In a way, the divorce has done the same thing. I didn't have any control over Mom and Dad's marriage, but once it fell apart, I regained my feeling of control by deciding where I wanted to live and by making a place for myself in both Mom's life and Dad's. This balance of control — I think it plays a huge role in my life. I feel pretty secure, pretty sure of myself. If I make mistakes I can fix them. Sometimes things do just happen, but I can <u>make</u> other things happen.

What do I hope to be doing in four years? Well, going off to college, of course. I think I'd like to go someplace far away, so that everything about college is different — different faces, a different part of the country. I want to have a taste of being really independent. I don't know what I want to study in college, though. Maybe something involving math? Or business? (I bet you're laughing at this now. I bet you're on your way to Connecticut College to study history or something.)

Well, Stacey-of-the-Future, as you read this I hope you remember that you were pretty happy when you were 13 years old, even while facing some difficulties. It hasn't always been easy, but overall, it's been good.

Love, Stacey

As I reread my letter one last time, I told myself that everything in it was true. And I tried to hold on to those positive thoughts about taking charge as my mind skipped ahead to graduation. Sure enough, both Dad and Samantha intended to be here for it. Dad would never miss it, of course, but Samantha had said that she wouldn't miss it either. They were going to drive to Stoneybrook on the day of graduation, spend the night in a hotel just outside of town, and drive back to NYC the next day. This wasn't ideal, but it wasn't bad either. With any luck, they wouldn't even see Mom. They'd sit rows and rows away from her, and hopefully she would be seated with the Thomas/Brewers or the Kishis, and she'd be so caught up in the ceremony that she wouldn't even think about Dad and his fiancée.

✳ Mary Anne

I don't know which is more satisfying — having finally talked with Logan or having finally finished my letter. Actually, yes I do. Finishing the letter was more satisfying. Talking with Logan was . . . well, it was as if a great weight had been lifted from my chest. It was a hugh relief. And after it was over, I felt almost exhilarated.

I'll get to that in a minute, though. First, here's my letter. (And what a struggle it was. writing it was almost like preparing for another final exam. But it was worth it.)

Dear Mary Anne,
Hello from four years ago. I can't believe you'll be a

senior in high school—
a graduating senior—
the next time you
read this. That sounds
so mature. And it
seems so far away.
I guess it is far away.
Four years ago you
were nine, four years
from now you'll be
on your way to
college.

If I had to pick the
single most defining
current event in my
life right now it
would be the fire. I
wonder if you'll still
feel that way by the
time you're reading
this. There have been
lots of other defining
events in my life,
and lately I have also
been thinking of all
the people in my life
who help to define
me, but if I had to

choose something recent with a great impact it would be the fire. Why? Because it changed so many things. There are the obvious changes, of course. The fire destroyed every possession we owned, except for what we were wearing that night. And afterward we spent almost a year living in flux — first with Kristy and her family, then in a rented house. Finally, we renovated the barn. So the fire certainly changed our living situation. Also, it made Dad and Sharon reexamine their careers.

But the fire did subtler things as well. At first it gave me

nightmares and a
lot of fears. But then
those fears somehow
changed into an
inner strength. (That
sounds so pompous.
You're probably laughing
at this part. But I
do think it's true.)
After awhile I didn't
want people worrying
and fussing over me.
I wanted to be strong
and independent, not
reliant on others. I
wanted to do things
for myself, take
action, take control.
        And this is what
led to Logan's and
my breakup. Logan
had been one of the
most important
people in my life
for quite some time,
but I felt he was
smothering me and
that I needed

breathing space. I didn't think we could work our problems out. So I broke up with him. And ever since that happened I have questioned it.

Is Logan still one of the most important people in your life? He might be. I had thought, after we broke up, that he would be out of my life forever. Just recently, though, I realized that he was very much unfinished business and that I needed to talk to him. So I did. Two days ago. Until now I had kept reminding myself that Logan and I are young.

That couples do not meet each other in middle school and stay together for the rest of their lives. But the truth is, occasionally they do.

So I'm awfully curious. Is Logan in your life now? If he is, what's going to happen? I know I want to go to college, and that's what Logan wants too. I doubt if we'll go to the same college, though. Logan will probably go to whatever school offers him an athletic scholarship. But I want to study psychology. I'm pretty sure of that. Oh, I wish I had a crystal ball and I could take a look at you reading this in the future, knowing the answers to some of these questions.

I feel as though I've strayed just a bit from what Mr. Kingbridge suggested we write about — especially from the subject of the people in my life and my changing family. But, well, this is what came out, and I think all of it is important.

By the way, in case you've forgotten, your thirteenth year was a tough one in lots of ways, but I think when you take a close look at it you'll see that you emerged from it stronger and definitely wiser, *thanks in large part to all those other people I meant to write about — Dad, Sharon, Dawn, Granny and Pop-pop, Grandma Baker, Kristy, Claudia, Stacey, Jessi, Mal, Abby. When things are tough, remember that, since these people or their memories will always be with you.*

Love,
Mary Anne

I didn't think I'd be embarrassed when I read the letter again in four years. In fact, I was proud of the letter. And very pleased that I had talked to Logan before I had written the final draft. I had actually asked him if he could meet me at Pizza Express one day after school. He hadn't sounded thrilled with the idea (no wonder, since I haven't been terribly friendly lately), but he had agreed. We sat in a booth in the back, so we had as much privacy as possible, and . . .

nothing earth-shattering happened, but at least we admitted that we don't like feeling mad, and that we especially don't like this business of not speaking to each other.

I am very relieved. If nothing else, when we run into each other we won't have to feel all uncertain and embarrassed. And we can start SHS on good terms. Maybe we'll even hang out every now and then. If we wind up with a couple of classes together next fall, that will be okay too. Nice, even.

❀ Claudia

Oh. My. Lord. Will finals ever be over? For days now I haven't done anything but study, study, study. Thank goodness for Stacey. She has been helping me almost every day with math and science. Here's the weird thing: I think I was more prepared for the math final than the science final. That must be a first. At least those two exams are OVER. In fact, only English is left. I take that one tomorrow and also will start finding out the results of my first exams.

I am SOOOOOO tired of looking at my English notes, though. So I am going to take a break here and write the letter to myself. I think I finally know what I want to say in it. And I had a fabulous idea for it. Instead of writing a regular letter I am going to interview myself.

Here goes.

Dear Claudia,

Hi, it's me, yourslef from the past. I have been thinking a LOT about this letter and what to say in it. It's a really hard letter to write. After lots of stoping and starting I desided to interview me as a way of writing the letter. Are you ready to hear about yourself from 4 yars ago? Interview person: So tell me Cladia who are the most important poeple in your life? me: In my life right now? Well, there are so many, but I' will try to narow them down. It might be intersting for you to see if they are still the most improtant poeple in your life when you read this letter. Frist and formost are my faimly — mom and Dad and Janine. And of course Peaches and Russ and Lynn. (As I write this Lynn is just a baby. She'll be getting ready for kindergraten by the time you read this again. Wierd.) And of course Mimi. Mimi will alway be important. Forever. She is a part of me she is with me. I wonder, do you still have pictures of her on your dresser? Then there are my freinds. My best freind use to be Stacey, and she is still a really really realy good freind but I guess not

my best freind anymore and I dont
know what we'll happen when we are in
high school. Kristy and Mary Anne are
close freinds too. I figure we'll always
know each other. Even if we don't hang
out and have the babysitters club in
high school I bet later on we' will send
each other pictures of are weddings and
our babies and stuff. And when I have
my frist big art show of course I will
invite them and thier familys.
Interviewer Person: Don't forget Alan.
Me: How could I forget Alan. Well I
don't realy think we'll still be together
in 4 yars. It's just such a long time
away. But Alan and I are having
fun now. I think we'll hang out over
the summer and then —
Excuse me, interviewer but could we not
talk about Alan now.
Interview person: Oh is Alan a sore
subject. Well we dont have to talk
about him. I will go on to the next
questoin. Lets talk about defining
events and things like that.
Me: Can I just tell you waht is most
improtant to me?
Interviewer Person: Okay.

Me: Well its my art. When I am working on a art projict I forget about all the bad things like flunking clases and never doing as well in school as Janine. I forget about staying back, repeating grades and being separated from my freinds.

Interview person: It sounds like you whant to talk about how hard school is for you.

Me: I love all kinds of art like sculpture and panting and drawing and making jewelry. I like ilustrating too. (there is a difference between illustrating and artwork I think.) I have even illustratted newslitters and flyers and such. Sometimes I just go to my room and pant and paint and paint. I get lost in the colors and shapes. Time flys by and I look at my watch and am surprized by how late it is.

Interviwer: What do you think you might be doing in four yars?

Me: I think I will be on my way to art school. In new york. I will study and paint and visit musums day and night. I

will think about where I will have my very frist show.
Interviewer person: Is there anything else you would like to add.
Me: I really realy hope I pass my finales so I can go on to SHS with my freinds next yar. I couldn't bare to be held back again.
Freindly Interview person: You' will pass them. Dont worry.
Me: Thank You.
Love, Claudia

That letter took so long to write that I had to finish it before school the next morning. (I was just determined to finish it and get it out of the way.) Then, the moment my letter and I arrived at school I ran to the office to pick up my first two graded exams — math and science. I took them politely from the secretary, walked daintily out of the office . . . and tore down the hall to the girl's room, where I could look at them in the privacy of a stall.

I opened the math exam first. At the top was a . . . C+. A C+!! I had passed. That wasn't a bad grade for math at all. In fact, it was a pretty good one. Thank you, Stacey, thank you. I let out an enormous sigh. Then I looked at the science exam.

When I saw the grade at the top my hands began to shake.

An F.

I had flunked science completely.

✳ Kristy

Every time I sat down to work on my letter I found myself going off in a different direction.

Time was running short. The letters were due in two days. And I had one more final left to study for. I decided just to sit down and write the letter. One draft. Whatever came out would be what wound up in the letter, what I would read in four years. I was feeling confined and needed to write in what I knew was called "stream of consciousness." (Being able to recall that term gave me high hopes for my last exam, which was English.)

And so . . . I pulled up a blank page on my computer screen and got to work.

Dear Kristy,
   I am writing this at a time in my life when I feel that everything is about to change. It oc-

curs to me that the next time you read this, everything will be about to change again. Right now, Charlie is going off to college (the first one of us Thomases to leave home), and I'll be starting high school in the fall. High school will bring <u>so many</u> changes. In four years, though, I'll be the one leaving for college, Sam will be in college, and Charlie will be graduating from college and going on to the rest of his adult life. Karen and David Michael will soon be sixth-graders, Andrew will be entering third grade, and Emily will be entering first grade. And a whole slew of new changes and challenges will be waiting.

Anyway, I don't care what Mr. Kingbridge said to write about. I just want to tell you about the Baby-sitters Club. Maybe the BSC will seem childish in four years. If it does, remind yourself that when you were in middle school, it was the most important thing in your life. Why? Because in many ways it was what connected so many other important things in your life.

When I think of the BSC I think of friends. Of course, Claudia and Mary Anne and I were already good friends when the BSC began, but the club drew us closer. And because of the BSC

I became friends with Dawn, Jessi, Abby, Stacey, and Mallory. Also Logan and Shannon. Plenty of adults and little kids became friends as well. A giant network of people. When I think about it, that network extends to California, to New York, even to Europe.

You know what? I have to admit something. I will admit it only once, and only here. The club is so important to me that I have been really hurt that it has changed and that it will probably change again. Whenever anybody dropped out of the club, even if it was because that person had to move away, I felt stung. And recently, when Abby and Jessi dropped out (after having already lost Dawn and Mal), and when Stacey, Claud, and Mary Anne said they could stay in the club but would have to scale back, I felt as if my world had fallen away. I know that sounds overly dramatic, especially since even I realized I couldn't devote quite as much time to baby-sitting anymore. But that is how I felt.

The Baby-sitters Club is my baby. It's my creation. I am SO proud of it. It may seem small and amateurish to some people, but it doesn't to me. It is the greatest thing I have done, and I must keep it alive. If it ends, a little part of me will die. And the worst thing is that no one understands this. Not even Mary Anne, who is my best friend in the world. I could explain it to her, and she might understand it intellectually, but she wouldn't <u>feel</u> it. Feeling it would be true understanding.

Why is the BSC not as important to anyone else as it is to me? Maybe in four years I'll have the answer to that. Right now I just feel as though I am standing at the edge of a cliff. I feel alone, and I feel scared, and I feel confused because I know I am the only one of my friends who feels this way. Everyone else is ready to move ahead, ready for high school, ready to move beyond the Baby-sitters Club. They're going to say good-bye to so many things so casually. And I'll be left standing at my cliff, afraid to fall, unable to turn around and go back. If only I had wings. Then I could soar into the sky. Maybe that's how my friends feel — as if they have wings. But not me.

So there we have it. I suppose the creation of the Baby-sitters Club was the defining event of my life. It must have been, if it's all I can write about now. I mean, here's my opportunity to write about Dad, about the impact his leaving had on our family and on my life, about how mad at him I've been. And here's my opportunity to write about what Watson's coming into our lives meant, about Emily's arrival. But all I can focus on is the Baby-sitters Club. Or maybe I'm obsessing about it. Who knows?

I don't want things to change now. I hope that in four years change will seem a more positive thing. I hope I'll be looking forward to going to college. When you read this letter again, remember that being thirteen can be really, really hard.

Love, Kristy

❀ Charlie

Dear Charlie,
   I can't believe you'll be
almost eighteen years old
when you read this letter.
How does it feel? I guess
that's a stupid question.
How does it feel to be
any age? I'm thirteen
years old now, and I
couldn't tell you how that
feels.
   But I can tell you about
my life and about some
parts of it that I am pretty
sure have affected me
forever. I'll start with the
basic stuff. I'm getting

ready to graduate from SMS. In the fall I'll be going to SHS. (That's where you'll be graduating from at the time you read this.) Sam is going into seventh grade in the fall, Kristy is going into fifth, and David Michael will still be in preschool.

It's been about three years since our father left us. Three very tough years. Mom has worked hard to support us. She has tried to do everything for us, and I don't mean that she has bought us a lot of stuff or taken us on a lot of trips or anything like that. I just mean, she has been a mom and a dad and she has held us all together. I think she is an amazing person. Mr. Kingbridge told us to write about defining events. Dad's leaving our family was definitely THE defining event in my life. So much changed after he took off. Mom worked long hours at her new job, which meant she couldn't be home after school. In the beginning that was the hardest part of all, because David Michael was just a baby. So Mom had to pay for his day care as well as everything else. And Sam and Kristy and I were on our own after school. I was in charge of Sam and Kristy, and it wasn't easy. But we managed. One thing I can say about us Thomases is that we pull together. Except for Dad. He is a jerk, a lazy jerk. But if his running away showed us how great we can be without him, then maybe it was worth it. I am really proud of myself for having helped Mom so much. I have done things that were not always fun, but I like feeling responsible. In fact, I think Sam and Kristy and I all became more responsible people because of Dad. Or because of non Dad. And, of course, because of Mom. She showed us how to be responsible.

I hope I am never as irresponsible as our father was. I take care of things, I finish things, I try to be on time, I keep promises, I try not to let people down, I work hard. Being responsible isn't easy, but I know how important it is. Being irresponsible is very easy, and its cruel to the people you love. Anyone can run away.

But not just anyone can stick around to take care of things, especially to take care of his family. If I have a family of my own one day, I will not abandon it. (By the way, I'm not saying people shouldn't get divorced, especially after they try to work things out. But I am saying they shouldn't run off without a word.) Just so you know, as I write this, we haven't heard from our father in almost a year. We don't even know exactly where he is.

What will my life be like in four years? Well, I guess I'll be going off to college, if we can afford it. Mom and I will probably have to look into scholarships. I wish I could go some-where really great like Harvard or Princeton, but those schools cost an arm and a leg. And I don't want someone else in the family to have to sacrifice something in order for me to go to college. Like, I don't want my going to college to mean that we can't afford to send Sam to college.

I Here are a few things I wish for the future:
That maybe Mom will be dating someone nice. She needs another important grown-up in her life.
That Kristy will stop taking herself so seriously.
That we won't have to pinch every single penny. Maybe I'll have a great job and can help Mom out. At least until I leave for college.
I don't know. I guess that's it. Have fun reading this letter again in four years.
—Charlie

From: NYCGirl
Subject: Burying the time capsule
To: MRDALI
Date: Wednesday, June 21
Time: 8:11:37 P.M.

Dear Ethan,
 Just two days until graduation! I can hardly believe it. I have such butterflies in my stomach. Good butterflies. I'm excited, but not nervous.
 Finals are over. We still haven't gotten all our exams back, though. Guess what. Claud has already flunked her science final. We're not sure what that will mean. Her parents are pretty upset and are going to have a meeting with some of her teachers tomorrow. I feel bad about the

exam, since I'd been tutoring Claud in science. On the other hand, I'd also been tutoring her in math and she passed that.

Keep your fingers crossed. Claud is terrified that she'll be held back again.

News of the day: We helped the kids bury the time capsule. I wasn't sure what to expect, but everyone has taken the project seriously and some very interesting things went into the capsule. I was actually kind of impressed. . . .

So much is going on. We arrived at school today thinking we would get the last of our finals back, only to find that the teachers need one more day with them, so we will have to wait until tomorrow. Poor Claud is practically dying. I'm a little nervous myself, since I have a shot at straight A's, although I didn't tell Claud that's why I'm nervous. Tomorrow we will also be issued our caps and gowns. And our yearbooks. Friday is . . . ta-da! . . . graduation. And, of course, Claud's party, if her parents aren't so mad that they decide she can't hold it.

For one miserable, miserable period of time earlier this week I thought that I myself would not be graduating. And all because of *Ribsy*. I had looked absolutely everywhere for that book. I had even looked in New York when I visited my dad over the weekend. I didn't expect to find it there, but you never know. Sometimes the contents of my closets are a considerable surprise to me. When, in the back of the one in the city, I unearthed a box that clearly had not been opened in quite some time, my heart leaped. I ripped it open and sifted through it, but no *Ribsy*. I did find a really nice pair of unworn socks, though.

On the train ride back to Stoneybrook on Sunday I tried to imagine how I would break the news to Mom that I would not be graduating (or that I would not be able to *attend* graduation — I wasn't sure which). When I pictured myself explaining that this all had to do with *Ribsy*, I figured Mom would either laugh at me or be furious. Neither response was appealing. Then something occurred to me, something that me think, *Stacey, you are the stupidest person in the world*. What I realized was that our librarian wouldn't care whether I gave him back the exact same copy of *Ribsy* that I took out two years ago. All he wants is a nice copy of the book for the library. The copy I checked out was probably a hardcover, so I could just go to the bookstore and buy a hardcover copy of *Ribsy* and hand it in to the librarian.

When I realized that, I almost burst out laughing. How could I possibly have thought I wouldn't graduate because I couldn't find some old copy of *Ribsy*?

On Monday after school I went to the bookstore downtown, bought *Ribsy*, and on Tuesday I gave it to our librarian. I handed it to him gift-wrapped, just in case he was in a bad mood or something. He accepted it with a grin and erased my name from a nasty-looking list in the computer.

Ahh. I could graduate.

And I could truly enjoy this afternoon's activity — the burying of the time capsule. At four o'clock, I cut through my backyard into Mal's and met up with her and her brothers and sisters. We walked to Mary Anne's house and found that a little crowd of kids was gathering. Of course, Kristy was already there. She was standing on the milk crate, wearing her visor. On a chain around her neck was her whistle. Next to the crate stood the empty popcorn tin.

"Hold on to your things until everyone has arrived!" she was yelling. "Don't put them in the box yet."

Everyone in the yard was clutching a paper bag or a package or an envelope. And if everyone felt the way I did, we were a pretty excited crowd.

"Hey!" Kristy called when she spotted Mal and me.

"Hi!" I called back.

I helped Kristy with crowd control for a few minutes. When we were pretty sure everyone had arrived, Kristy cupped her hands to her mouth and shouted, "Welcome! Thank you for coming. This is going to be a great time capsule. Now, the first thing we have to do is dig a hole to bury it in."

The Pike triplets were prepared for this and got to work with shovels near an herb garden behind Mary Anne's new house. While they dug, the other kids and my friends, one by one, stepped up to the tin box and dropped into it whatever they had brought. If they felt like saying a few words, they did.

"Here's a Krushers' softball," said Jackie.

"I cut out a newspaper article," said Jessi.

"This is one of our old BSC fliers," said Kristy.

"I'm putting in our school newspaper," said Charlotte. "Stacey, read this first, though, okay?"

Charlotte handed the newspaper to me instead of dropping it into the tin, and while the other kids continued to step forward, I read what she was pointing to. It was an essay she had written for school about an important person in her life. And she had chosen me as her important person.

"Charlotte, thank you," I told her. "I don't know what to say."

"That's okay," she replied. "When you're almost-sisters, you don't always have to say everything. Sometimes you just know."

I gave Charlotte a hug, and we turned back to the kids gathered around the box in time to see Claire drop her old teddy bear into it.

"Claire, are you sure you want to put Ba-ba in there?" said Kristy.

"That's what I've been asking her all along," Vanessa whispered.

Kristy glanced at Mal, who simply shrugged. Ba-ba went into the capsule with everything else.

By the time the capsule had been filled, the hole had been dug. Kristy lugged the box to the edge of the hole and, with great ceremony, placed it inside. "On this day, the twenty-first of June," she said, "the citizens of Stoneybrook hereby bury a time capsule, not to be opened for seven years. At which time, Byron, Jordan, and Adam Pike" — Kristy motioned for them to stand beside her — "will be in charge of digging it up."

"I hope they remember where it's buried," I heard Nicky whisper to Vanessa.

"And now, who will throw the first handful of dirt in the hole?" asked Kristy.

"You, Kristy, you!" cried several of the kids.

So Kristy threw in a handful of dirt, and the rest of the kids followed suit. I noticed that Claire looked horrified as the tin slowly disappeared, but she said nothing.

A few minutes later, our time capsule officially buried, we began to walk home.

❋ Mary Anne

Thursday, June 22
Dear Diary,
Today got off to
an unexpected start
when the phone rang
before Dad and
Sharon and I had
even sat down to
breakfast. Dawn and
Jeff flew in last
night and they were
still asleep, jet-lagged.
(I hoped the phone
wouldn't wake them.)
I thought the caller
might be Kristy, but

*it was Claire. And
she was upset.
    Guess what. She
wanted Ba-ba back . . . .*

Sharon was the one who answered the phone.
She was edging around the breakfast table with a
plate of toast, and she was right in front of the phone
when it rang. "Hello?" she said, grabbing it before it
could ring again. I knew she wanted Dawn and Jeff
to be able to sleep as late as possible. Then, "What?
. . . What?" After a moment, she handed the phone
to me. "Mary Anne, I think it's for you." When I
raised my eyebrows at her, she added, "I'm not sure
who it is."

"Hello?" I said.

The voice on the other end was tearful. What
I heard was, "Wawaaa . . . be . . . can't . . . Ba-
ba . . ."

"Claire? Is that you?"

"Yeeeeeess!" A wail.

"What's the matter? Is Mal there?"

There was a clunk as the phone was set down.
Then someone said hello.

"Mrs. Pike? This is Mary Anne."

Mrs. Pike sounded crabby. It turned out she

hadn't had a whole lot of sleep the night before. Neither, I was guessing, had the rest of the Pikes. Claire had awoken shortly after midnight and had discovered that she couldn't sleep without Ba-ba next to her.

"Uh-oh," I said.

"Mary Anne, here's Mal. I'm going to let you talk to her."

Mal sounded as crabby as Mrs. Pike.

"What do you want to do?" I finally asked her.

"I think we're going to have to dig up the time capsule."

"Dig it up?! Kristy will kill us."

"I know, but we have to do it. Claire needs Ba-ba, and she knows where she is. We can't just leave her buried in the ground."

I looked at my watch. "Okay. Can Claire wait until after school, though? We don't have time to do it now. Plus, I kind of think Kristy will want to be present for this."

"Whatever," Mal replied crossly. "Anyway, Claire has morning kindergarten for some reason today."

As I had suspected, Kristy was none too pleased with the idea of digging up the time capsule. "We just buried it!" she exclaimed.

159

We were standing in the hallway by Kristy's locker.

"I know, but Claire is desperate," I explained.

It was Kristy's turn to become crabby. "All right," she said gruffly. "Right after school today." She turned and walked off, muttering under her breath, "Whoever heard of digging up a time capsule twenty-four hours later?"

"Can't you just pretend you buried it today instead of yesterday?" I called after her.

"No!"

I decided not to let anyone else's crabby mood ruin my day. It was one of our last days at SMS and I intended to enjoy it. Everywhere the eighth-graders were lounging around with their yearbooks, leisurely signing them. The sixth- and seventh-graders were in their classrooms working away at who knew what, but us eighth-graders were DONE! Classes were over. We were here to get our final exams, to clean out our lockers, to sign yearbooks, to have a rehearsal for graduation . . .

The moment homeroom was over I tore down to the main office to get back my last two final exams — social studies and French. Ha! An A on the French exam and a B+ on the social studies. I was going to end my career at SMS with nearly straight A's. Not bad. Not bad at all.

Even better, as far as I was concerned, was that Logan and I didn't feel we had to avoid each other anymore. In fact, when I spotted him in the hall just before lunch we waved and called hi.

When the final bell rang that day, Kristy found me signing another yearbook. "I'll walk home with you," she said.

"Cool. Dawn can help us dig up the capsule."

Kristy made a face.

"Oh, for heaven's sake," I said. "It isn't that bad, Kristy. Nobody else is going to want anything from the time capsule. All we have to do is open it, take Ba-ba out, close it up again, and bury it. This time it really won't be opened for seven years."

"I guess."

Kristy's mood improved on our walk home because she was excited about seeing Dawn.

"Plus, now Dawn can look in the capsule," I pointed out. (Dawn had mailed an envelope to me to put in the time capsule since she wasn't going to be at the official burial.)

"True," said Kristy.

Kristy and Dawn had a happy reunion when we reached my house. They hugged and laughed, and

Dawn said she couldn't wait to see us graduate the next day.

"You're going to get to see the time capsule too," I told her, and explained what had happened.

Ten minutes later, Mallory showed up with Claire, Nicky, and Vanessa. Mal and Dawn had a happy reunion of their own.

Then Nicky said gleefully, "I want to see if worms are crawling all over Ba-ba."

Claire burst into tears, and Mal put an arm around her. "It's a *sealed metal* container, Nicky," she said. "There won't be any worms in it now, and there won't be any worms in it seven years from now."

"Oh." Nicky looked disappointed.

"All right, let's get going," said Kristy.

"Hurry!" cried Claire.

Mal, Dawn, Kristy, and I set to work with shovels and trowels, and a few minutes later the tin box was in view. We hauled it out of the ground and Kristy stood over it, shaking her head. Finally she announced, "The unofficial opening of the Stoneybrook time capsule." She pried off the lid and pawed through the contents until she spotted Ba-ba's ears. Then she reached in, pulled her out, and handed her to Claire, who hugged Ba-ba to her chest.

162

"Thank you," said Mal.

"You're welcome." Kristy put the lid back on the tin and returned the tin to the hole. "Now," she said, standing up and brushing dirt off the knees of her jeans, "the people of Stoneybrook once again bury their time capsule, and this time it really, really, REALLY is not going to be opened for seven years."

When the box had completely disappeared under the earth Kristy looked at the plot of loose soil and said, "We ought to make a marker to put here so we know exactly where the capsule is buried. That might be a nice project for the summer."

A marker *was* a nice idea, but how could Kristy even think about such things when graduation was . . . the next day? I watched Mal and the Pikes amble home, Claire still clutching Ba-ba, and I turned to Kristy and Dawn. I pictured my friends and myself in our caps and gowns. I imagined the events the next day would bring. We would become SMS graduates. Middle school would be over. We would be on our way to high school.

❄ Claudia

From: ckishi
Subject: GARDUATION!
To: NYCGirl
Date: Thursday, June 22
Time: 9:09:53 P.M.

Stacey can you beleive it I am going to graduate with you guys after all.!! All I have to do is pass sumer school and I have passed summer school before. Also I pased all my other finales so I realy didnt do so badly. And now on to tomorrow I am SOOOOOOOO excited. Actual garduation! And then the party here. Oh you know what I am just way too exited to finish this e-mail. I have to call you. I am going to call you right now.

It was a little too much for me. Considering the incredibly bad start the day had gotten off to, I had not had high hopes for much of anything. In the past, meetings between my parents and my teachers have led to horrifying turns of events. When I headed off to SMS on Thursday morning, knowing Mom and Dad would soon be doing the same thing, I fully expected them (or my guidance counselor or somebody) to inform me later that I was going to have to repeat eighth grade. If that had happened, well, I just wasn't sure what my response would have been. I think I might have had a tantrum right there in the hallway. All day long I was on pins and needles. From 10:00 until 11:00, the time of the Meeting About Me, I kept an eye out for my parents. I didn't see them, though, and by the beginning of the last period of the day I hadn't heard anything from anyone. I was so nervous that my skin began to itch and I wished I could crawl out of it.

You can imagine my reaction when I heard my name called over the loudspeaker, summoning me to the office. I practically ran there. I was so desperate for news then that I almost didn't care whether it was good or bad. (Well, not really, but you know what I mean.) Anyway, I bolted into the office and was greeted there by my guidance counselor. And guess what, I may have flunked my science final, but I was going to be allowed to graduate with my friends. I'd have to take science in summer school, though, and my diploma would be a blank piece of paper. But I didn't care. That blank will be replaced with the real thing when I pass the summer-school course. (Of course, if I don't pass it I really will have to repeat eighth grade, but I am going to do everything I can think of to pass it. I KNOW I'll be going to SHS in September with my friends.)

So . . . how did I spend the rest of the afternoon? Shopping. I'd been too superstitious to buy anything for the party until I knew whether I'd be graduating myself. Now I had a million things to do. Which was good, because I was becoming overly excited about graduation, and planning the party kept my mind off of it.

The next thing I knew, it was Friday morning. The eighth-graders didn't have to go to school until two-thirty — half an hour before graduation. Janine was at school, Mom and Dad were at work, Stacey and her mom had decided to go to the hairdresser to-gether, Mary Anne was busy with Dawn . . . I was on my own, but I had things to do. I cleaned up my room, then decorated it for the party. And slowly the morning passed. Mom came home from work early to help me get ready for the ceremony, and at 2:20 we were in the car on the way to SMS.

Mom asked me a hundred questions. Did I know where to meet her and Dad and Janine after graduation? (Yes.) Was I ready for the party? (Yes.) Had I called Peaches to tell her where she and Russ should meet Mom and Dad? (Yes.) Had I remembered my cap and gown? (Yes. Duh.)

I couldn't wait to get out of the car. We found a mob scene at school. The parking lot was full — of cars and of people.

"How am I going to find Stacey?" I wailed. And like magic, she materialized at my elbow then.

"Oh, my lord, I am so nervous!" she cried.

"Me too!" Suddenly we were hugging each other. "Do you remember where we're supposed to go now?"

"The gym," she replied. "Come on."

" 'Bye, Mom," I said. "Go get good seats. We'll see you later."

Stacey and I, clutching the boxes containing our caps and gowns, made our way to the gym. We were unbelievably keyed up. So was everyone we passed.

"An hour from now we'll be graduates!"

"SHS, here we come!"

"We're almost out of here!"

When we reached the gym, Stacey and I looked around for Kristy, Abby, and Mary Anne. We wouldn't be sitting together during graduation since we would be seated alphabetically, but we had agreed to meet in the gym anyway. That was where we would put on our caps and gowns, and where we would line up to march to the playing fields for the ceremony.

"There's Abby," said Stacey.

"There are Kristy and Mary Anne," I said.

The five of us drew into a knot and hugged one another.

"Come on," said Mary Anne. "We better get ready."

We put on our gowns and adjusted our caps and tassels.

"We get to keep the tassels, you know," said Abby. "Look. They have little gold SMS charms on them."

"May I have your attention?" A voice boomed through a megaphone. The gym fell silent. "Time to line up. Alphabetically, please. Try to remember who you were standing next to when we rehearsed this yesterday."

"Well, this is it," I said to my friends. "We'll meet up afterward, okay?"

Unexpectedly, Kristy burst into tears.

She started a chain reaction.

"Not now, you guys," said Abby, searching for a tissue. "We have to pull ourselves together. We don't want to look all blotchy when we get our diplomas."

After a lot of sniffling and hugging we calmed down. We found our places in a line of blue robes that wound around the gym. From outside came the sound of our school band tuning up (minus all its eighth-grade members, of course), and before I knew it, I was marching through the halls of SMS. We left the building through a side door and snaked around to the back of the school. Before us was a sea of folding chairs. Every single one of them was filled and a small crowd of people was standing behind them. My classmates were filing onto risers. I followed Stephanie Kingsley to our spot in the third row. Then I turned and faced the audience. I tried to find my family, but the crowd was too big.

When the last of my classmates was in place, the music stopped and our principal, Mr. Taylor, stepped up to the podium and made a brief speech. This was followed by several more speeches — our class officers spoke, and Emily Bernstein gave the valedictory address.

And then . . . at last . . .

"It is now time to award the diplomas," said Mr. Taylor when he had returned to the mike.

My classmates began to file off of the bleachers. As each one reached the podium, Mr. Kingbridge announced his or her name and Mr. Taylor handed out the diploma. When my name was called I heard a shout from the audience (my parents? shouting with relief?) and I grabbed my cap off of my head and waved it in the air. I had done it! I had graduated! (Sort of.)

The ceremony flew by. Before I knew it, my classmates and I were standing in our spots on the bleachers again. After a moment of silence, Mr. Taylor looked at us, each holding a diploma, and said proudly, "Ladies and gentlemen, our graduates."

I have never in my life heard such cheering and clapping. Every single one of us was grinning. I was still grinning a few minutes later when my friends and I had filed off of the bleachers once again, this time to find our friends and families in the crowd.

"Claudia! Claudia!"

I heard someone shout my name. Then I was being wrapped in a hug. Mary Anne.

She started to cry, of course, and so did I.

The next half an hour was complete pandemonium. I found my parents and I remember introducing them to Samantha, when she and Mr. McGill were walking around looking for Stacey. Jessi and Mal were there. And at one point or another I think I saw every member of every one of my friends' families.

Eventually we started taking pictures.

"Photo op!" Abby cried. "First the graduates."

Snap. Someone took a picture of Mary Anne, Kristy, Abby, Stacey, and me.

Snap. A picture of me with Mom, Dad, Janine, Peaches, Russ, and Lynn.

Snap. A picture of Kristy and her huge family.

Snap. A (harmonious) picture of Stacey and her parents *and* Samantha.

"Okay, now all the BSC members!" called Kristy.

Snap. A picture of Kristy, Stacey, Jessi, Abby, Dawn, Mary Anne, Mal, and me.

I think the picture-taking could have gone on for quite some time, but eventually I began to feel overwhelmed by the crowd. I drew Kristy aside. "Don't you guys want to go to my house now?"

Kristy looked a little overwhelmed herself. "Definitely," she said.

"Come on, everybody." I rounded up Abby, Mal, Mary Anne, Dawn, Jessi, and Stacey.

"Wait," said Kristy as we were getting ready to

171

leave. "I think we need one more picture of the eight of us. The BSC members — without our caps and gowns, though."

"Why?" asked Dawn.

"Because I want one picture to remind me of us as we used to be," said Kristy. "Before some of us graduated and everything changed."

A pause. Then, "Okay," I said. "Hey, Janine! One more picture!"

Snap.

When I looked at that picture later, after Janine had had her film developed, I saw one of the most somber pictures ever taken of the eight of us. But I framed it and put it on my desk.

❀ Kristy

June 23

almost don't know what to say here. It's midnight. Midnight of day we graduated. Midnight of day my life changed. It's over. It's all over. Shouldn't feel that way, really. Think am supposed to feel happier.

My friends and I were driven to Claudia's in two cars. Charlie drove Stacey, Abby, Jessi, and me there in the Junk Bucket. And Claudia's uncle Russ and her aunt Peaches, who have a van, dropped off Claud and the others.

"Okay, PAAAAARTY!!" cried Claudia as we

met on her front lawn. The rest of us began to cheer and whistle. Even me. I hadn't expected to feel excited, exactly. But I found that I did. Everyone else's excitement was contagious.

"Whoooooo, we did it!" cried Stacey.

"I can't believe you guys get to go on to high school next year," said Jessi enviously.

"Oh, look who's talking. The person who's going to travel the world this summer!" said Dawn.

"But I'll be left all alone at SMS," Jessi complained.

Mal put her arm around her. "You'll survive. At least you won't be a lowly sixth-grader anymore. Seventh grade is much cooler."

"Well, I still can't wait for high school," said Jessi.

"It's going to be pretty exciting," said Mary Anne.

"Yeah, older guys," said Claudia.

"Better dances," said Stacey.

"Better everything, I bet," added Mary Anne.

Claud wanted to start the party. "Let's go inside, you guys," she said, opening her front door. "Come on upstairs."

We trooped up the stairs to Claud's room. I tried to pretend we were about to begin a BSC meeting, just like one of the ones we would have held a few months ago. But when I saw the inside of Claud's room that idea flew out the window. Claud had turned it into a graduation fantasyland. Bunches of balloons were tied everywhere. Streamers crisscrossed the ceiling. A HAPPY GRADUATION! sign was strung up over her bed. (Well, actually, the sign said, HAPPY GARDUATION!) The desk was covered with a paper cloth decorated with caps and gowns and diplomas, and strewn with sequins and glitter. On it Claud was setting out sodas and a bowl of punch and plates of cookies and chips and popcorn and veggies and even tiny chocolate diplomas.

"Pop one of the balloons," Claud directed me, handing me a pin.

Popping balloons has never been one of my favorite activities, but I obeyed and was showered with more sequins and glitter.

"Cool!" exclaimed Mal. "How did you do that?"

Claud just shrugged and grinned, while the rest of us set to work popping balloons. Soon we were covered with glitter. We were shaking it out of our hair and brushing it off of our clothes.

"Look at us!" I exclaimed.

"We are . . . the Baby-sitters Club!" cried Mary Anne.

We abandoned the pins and flopped on Claud's bed and the floor.

"Remember the time Jackie got a raisin stuck up his nose?" Stacey suddenly said.

My friends and I began to laugh.

"And he got his arm stuck in his pants drawer?" I added.

"Remember when he hit the home run that broke a window at Stoneybrook Elementary?" said Mal.

"Think of all the stuff that's happened since we formed the Baby-sitters Club," said Claud.

"Yeah, Lucy Newton was born," said Dawn.

"We learned sign language so we could communicate with Matt Braddock," said Jessi.

"Dawn and I became stepsisters!" exclaimed Mary Anne.

"Yeah, a lot of non-baby-sitting stuff has happened too," said Dawn.

"Tons," agreed Stacey. "I don't think I would have gotten through most of it without you guys."

"I know I wouldn't have," said Mary Anne.

"Yes, you would have," said Abby.

"Not as well. You guys are the best friends in the world." Mary Anne's eyes filled with tears.

"We've had a lot of fights, though," I pointed out.

"Being friends doesn't mean we can't fight," said Stacey. She glanced ever so briefly at Claudia. Then she added, "Actually, you just never know about fighting and getting along. Did you guys see Mom and Dad and Samantha all together this afternoon? I nearly fainted."

"That was kind of amazing," agreed Jessi.

"Remember how mad you were when I decided to go to Riverbend?" Mal said to Jessi.

"I'll never forget it."

"Remember the fight Dawn and I had after Dad and Sharon got married?" Mary Anne spoke up.

"Sometimes fighting makes friendships stronger," said Stacey.

"Does everyone here think we'll still be friends when we're grown-up?" Claudia asked.

"Oh, please, do we have to talk about that?" I said. "I don't want to think about us *not* being friends."

Mary Anne was sprawled on the bed with a fist-ful of popcorn. "Well, I want to tell you what I think anyway," she said. "Because it might make you feel better, Kristy. See, to be honest, I'm not sure that when we're grown-up we'll be exactly the kind of friends we are now — "

"Well, that is exactly what I don't want to hear," I interrupted.

"Shh, just listen," said Mary Anne impatiently. *"But,"* she went on, "I do think we'll always be friends. You know, my dad has friends from his childhood. They may not be his best, best friends, but they are people he knew in elementary school — there's even one person he knew in preschool — and they still write letters to each other, and send e-mail and Christmas cards, and meet up sometimes."

"My mom's best friend now," said Jessi, "was her best friend from when she was growing up. They've been best friends since they were four years old."

"That is so cool," I said, feeling reassured.

Jessi grinned. "Yeah. You know, when they were six they decided they were going to become famous actresses and stay together for the rest of their lives. They were going to marry twin brothers and have their kids at the same time and all live in one big house."

My friends and I burst out laughing.

"Well, we know what your mom is doing now," said Mal. "What about her best friend?"

"She's an architect in Chicago, and she's married but she and her husband don't have any kids. But she and Mom are *still* best friends. They constantly talk on the phone, and they see each other about two times a year."

"Maybe being a best friend is different when you're grown-up than when you're a kid," said Abby. "I mean, just because you *are* a grown-up."

"When I'm grown-up," said Claud, "when I finally get out of school and become an artist, a *real* artist, I don't think I'll want to get married right away. I think I'll just want to be an artist and live on my own for awhile. Then maybe I'll get married."

"I'm not sure I want to get married at all," I said. "I don't see why everyone has to get married."

"Everyone doesn't have to get married," replied Stacey.

"They do if they want kids."

"They do not. Plenty of people who aren't married have kids."

"Oh, good. Then I want to adopt four kids but not get married. Maybe I'll adopt five. You know I'll want to have a lot of kids."

"I want to get married *and* have kids," said Mal. "But not eight kids. I think just two or three. I'll want to have my writing career too."

"When you are a famous dancer, Jessi, traveling the world, will you come back and visit your old friends?" asked Mary Anne.

"Of course I will. And when I'm not around, I'll send all of you lots and lots of postcards and letters and e-mail."

"Hey, Dawn," I said. (I was beginning to feel more relaxed. This wasn't such a bad conversation after all.) "Do you think you'll stay in California all your life?"

"I don't know. I might. Well, probably. But you never know. I think I'd like to go to college here in the East. Maybe. But then go back to California. And you know what? I'm pretty sure I want to get married someday, but I'm not sure I want kids."

"You're kidding. Why not?" asked Abby.

"I don't think I'd be a good parent. I mean, I like kids and everything, but I don't know that I want to have any of my own."

"Not everyone has to have kids," said Jessi. "My mom's friend is really happy and she doesn't have kids. But I think I want to have at least one."

"Well, I'll tell you guys something," said Abby. "I know for sure that before I settle down in any way, I want to see this whole big world. You are so lucky, Jessi. Traveling around. Visiting foreign countries. I wish I could see every country there is. I want to do lots of traveling as soon as I can."

"Hey, you guys. What do you want to do?" I asked Mary Anne and Stacey.

"I don't know," said Mary Anne. "I really don't. Not what I want to do or whether I want to get married or anything. I think I just want to enjoy high school and college first."

"Well, I know for sure that I want to go into some kind of business," said Stace. "Like, run a big company, or own a store or a chain of stores. Working with my mom will be good practice. And I guess I want to get married and have kids, but I haven't thought much about it."

"You know what?" I said. "We should make a pact."

"What kind of pact?" asked Dawn.

"That in twelve years, when we're all grown-up and out of college, we'll meet — the eight of us — and have a reunion. Then we can see what we're really doing."

"Where will we meet?" Abby asked.

"I don't know," I said. "We can't decide that now. But we should write this up and make it official — that on January first, twelve years from now, we will all call one another and plan a reunion, some-where, for the eight of us on June twenty-third of that year."

We were silent for a few moments, considering this. Then, very solemnly, Claud took a piece of paper and a pen from her desk drawer and handed them to Mary Anne, our secretary, who drafted an official-looking pact. She promised to have it copied for each of us the next day.

When the party ended that evening, I went home thinking of the pact. And I began to think about it again, much later, as I was writing in my journal.

Have just spent last few minutes reliving entire party. Thought of pact makes me happier. Am fairly certain that even though our friendships may change as we get older, we will always remain friends, the eight of us.

Friends forever.

The End

Dear Readers,

It's hard to believe, but it's been almost fifteen years since Kristy, Claudia, Mary Anne, and Stacey formed the Baby-sitters Club. When I first began working on the series, I thought I was going to write four books, one about each of the girls. But to my surprise, a total of 213 books about Kristy and her friends followed. I've had a lot of fun working on the series; in fact, these have been fifteen fabulous years. But now it's time to say good-bye to the members of the BSC.

The series wouldn't have lasted so long without the support of many people, but especially without you — the loyal BSC readers. Over the years, I've felt a great connection to my readers. I've received thousands of amazing letters — letters with suggestions for plots, letters of thanks, and letters from kids who simply wanted to share their lives with me. I've met readers at book signings, at schools, and through contests. Of all the wonderful things that happened to me as a result of the Baby-sitters Club, getting to know my readers was one of the best.

I've been thinking a lot about decisions and choices lately. Often, making the right decision is easy. But sometimes a decision is difficult to make, even when you feel certain it's the right one. That's how I feel about the decision to end the series. I will miss working on the books, miss spending time with the characters, and especially miss my connection with the BSC fans. On the other hand, I have fifteen years of memories, many of them created by you. That's why this last book is dedicated to my readers.

Thank you for your loyalty and enthusiasm.

Happy reading,

Ann M. Martin

The History of the BSC

1985

1985
Scholastic editor Jean Feiwel sits down with author Ann M. Martin and shares the idea for the Baby-sitters Club.
Ann signs on to write a four-book series.

November – 1985
First BSC book due from Ann to Scholast[ic]

August - 1986
Kristy comes up with
the idea for the Baby-sitters Club.
She, Claudia, Mary Anne, and Stacey
are the founding members.

December - 1986
Readers learn
"the truth about Stacey"
— that she has diabetes.

1986

August - 1986
Kristy's Great Idea
is published!

July - 1987
Kristy's mom marries Watson Brewer. Kristy and her stepsister, Karen, are bridesmaids.

November - 1987
Boy-crazy Stacey and Mary Anne head to Sea City for the first time.

1987

January - 1987
The BSC is so successful that the four-book series is expanded.

Fall - 1987
Each BSC book published this fall hits #1 on the best-seller list!

May - 1988
Stacey moves back to New York City with her parents. Her friends in the BSC are crushed.

February - 1988
Mary Anne meets Logan Bruno...and her life is never the same again.

June - 1988
Hello, Mallory and Jessi! The BSC has two new members.

1988

February - 1988
The BSC books come out monthly for the first time.

July - 1988

The first BSC Super Special, *Baby-sitters on Board!*, is published.

August - 1988

The first Baby-sitters Little Sister book, *Karen's Witch*, is published.

1988

Spring/Summer - 1988

BSC Fan Club is launched!

December - 1988

The *Los Angeles Times Book Review* writes, "Martin's number one book is outselling the number one books on the adult fiction a nonfiction lists." In other word the BSC is HUGE.

January - 1989
Kristy starts a kids' softball team, Kristy's Krushers.

July - 1989
The Baby-sitters Club members head to Camp Mohawk for a summer they'll never forget.

August - 1989
Claudia's beloved grandmother Mimi dies.

October - 1989
Stacey moves back to Stoneybrook after her parents split up.

1989

February - 1989
The front page of the *USA Today* Life section proclaims, "Young readers love 'Baby-sitters'"!

April - 1989
Nine BSC books hit the B. Dalton Top 20 best-seller list.

September - 1990
Dawn falls for Travis, an older boy. Complications ensue.

December - 1990
The BSC members w the Jack o' Lottery a visit Dawn's dad ar brother in Californi

January - 1990
Dawn's mom and Mary Anne's dad get married. Dawn and Mary Anne become stepsisters.

1990

May - 1990
Mary Anne and Too Many Boys is one of the fastest-selling BSC books in history, selling over 800,000 copies in just eight months!

March - 1990
Over 20,000,000 BSC books in print!

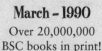

Fall - 1990
Ann M. Martin starts the Ann M. Martin Foundatio dedicated to benefiting child education and literacy progra and homeless people and anim

May - 1991
The BSC's biggest baby-sitting job ever, when they throw a sleepover for 100 kids.

August - 1991
Romance lives! Mary Anne and Logan are back together again.

February - 1991
Mary Anne and Logan break up!

September - 1991
Mallory goes on strike.

1991

Spring - 1991
The BSC TV series premieres on HBO. Later the videos of the series will hit best-seller charts.

August - 1991
America's favorite baby-sitters are detectives, too! The first BSC Mystery, *Stacey and the Missing Ring*, hits the stores and is an immediate success.

December - 1991
BSC has the top three books on the *Publishers Weekly* best-seller list. For 1991, 10 of the top 16 best-sellers of the year are BSC books, each selling over 300,000 copies.

June - 1991
BSC Super Special #6, *New York, New York!*, is illustrated by Ann's father, Henry R. Martin.

May – 1992
Everyone in Stoneybrook is worried when Jake Kuhn disappears.

February – 1992
Stacey's New York best friend, Laine Cummings, comes to visit Stoneybrook …and it's a total disaster.

1992

March – 1992
The BSC now includes videos, trading cards, calendars, and a board game!

June – 1992
The *Chicago Tribu* declares, "Move o Nancy Drew: You readers have a lo more in common w the Baby-sitters Clu

June – 1992
You wanted to get to know him better… and you did! *Logan's Story*, the first BSC Special Edition Readers' Request book, is published.

September – 1992
Dawn saves the planet
(or at least tries to).

December – 1992
Mary Anne has a
makeover. Logan swoons.

1992

Fall – 1992
Over 1,000 real-life Baby-sitters Clubs
exist in 48 states across the USA.

November – 1992
Ann, her editor Bethany,
and members of the BSC
ride in the Macy's
Thanksgiving Day Parade.

September – 1992
n what day of the week
d Kristy get the idea for
e BSC? If you know the
swer is Tuesday, then the
*BSC Trivia and Puzzle
Book* (published this
month) is for you.

May - 1993

He's smart...he's handsome ...he's 22! Stacey falls for her substitute math teacher.

October - 1993

Mallory comes down with mono. (And she didn't even get it from Ben Hobart!)

1993

January - 1993

The BSC now has over 50,000,000 books in print!

Summer - 1993

The BSC sponsors a "Get Involved" contest inviting readers to talk about improving their communities. More than 12,000 entries are received.

November - 1993

Now readers can learn all of the BSC's sitting secrets — *The Baby-sitters Club Guide to Baby-sitting* is now available.

December - 1994
Here come the bridesmaids! Dawn's dad marries Carol, while on the other side of the USA, Stacey is a bridesmaid for Mrs. Barrett.

June - 1994
Big trouble on Fire Island! Stacey gets caught on a secret rendezvous with her boyfriend Robert.

1994

January - 1994
The BSC is now translated into more than 19 languages, in countries as different as Norway, Indonesia, and Israel.

July - 1994
The release of *The Baby-sitters Remember* marks a big 100,000,000 books in print for the BSC!

November - 1994
The first BSC Portrait Collection, *Stacey's Book*, hits bookstores.

February - 1994
The BSC Boutique opens at FAO Schwartz in New York City, kicking off Ann's BSC World Tour.

Summer – 1995
The BSC experience supreme spookiness when they visit a haunted house.

October – 1995
Abby Stevenson joins the BSC.

March – 1995
One of the biggest feuds in BSC history begins when Stacey starts hanging out with a crowd of bad girls.

August – 1995
Farewell, Dawn! Dawn decides to leave Stoneybrook and move to California for good.

1995

March – 1995
The BSC Mall Tour begins.

Fall – 1995
Ann sets off on the fifty-state BSC Across the USA Tour.

August – 1995
Lights! Camera! Baby-sitting! The Baby-sitters Club movie premieres in theaters across America.

September – 1995
It's a whole new look for the BSC!

March - 1996
Is it love? Kristy and Bart confront their complicated feelings for each other.

June - 1996
Kristy faces off against her archenemy, Cary Retlin, in a mystery war.

October - 1996
Who says spelling doesn't count? Claudia is sent back to seventh grade.

1996

January - 1996
The BSC starts its tenth year on the *Publishers Weekly* best-seller list.

September - 1996
BSC #100, *Kristy's Worst Idea*, is an instant best-seller!

Fall - 1996
The first BSC CD-ROM is released and the BSC website, *www.scholastic.com/babysitters-club*, is launched.

July - 1997
Coast-to-coast fun! The BSC road-trips across the country.

December - 1997
Mary Anne gets a job as a department store elf.

1997

July - 1997
The BSC Fan Club has over 60,000 members.

August - 1997
Ann M. Martin's California Diaries series debuts.

July – 1998
Viva La Sitters!
The BSC heads to Europe.

1998

February – 1998
The BSC Mysteries get a new design.

Fall – 1998
The BSC is named one of the Books of the Century by the *New York Times Book Review*.

May – 1999
Big changes are coming when Mary Anne's house is destroyed by a fire.

August – 1999
Kristy goes to California to see her long-lost father get remarried.

January – 1999
Mallory starts her new life when she heads off to boarding school.

October – 1999
It's time to move on: Mary Anne breaks up with Logan.

1999

July – 1999
The BSC Friends Forever series begins with *Everything Changes*.

Spring – 1999
The BSC now has over 150,000,000 copies in print.

February - 2000
Claudia and Stacey's big fight (over a boy) ends... with a surprise twist.

October - 2000
Can it be possible that Claudia's dating Alan Gray?!?

November - 2000
Kristy, Claudia, Mary Anne, and Stacey graduate from Stoneybrook Middle School.

2000

November - 2000
The last BSC book, *Graduation Day*, is published. There are now over 180,000,000 BSC books in print.

The Baby-sitters Club Index

Number of BSC and BSC Friends Forever books: 145
Number of BSC Super Specials, Portrait Collections, and
   Special Editions: 28
Number of BSC Mysteries: 40
Total number of BSC books: 213

Total number of pages in these 213 books: 31,570
Number of hours it would take to read these books (assuming
   one page per minute): 526.17
Number of nonstop reading days it would take: 21.92

If you put one of each BSC paperback into a stack, its height
   would be: 7.5 feet
Average height of a thirteen-year-old girl: 5.25 feet

First printing of BSC #1, *Kristy's Great Idea*: 35,000 copies
As of March 2000, number of BSC and BSLS books in print:
   176,539,000
Number of inches these books would stretch if you lined them
   up vertically: 1,346,109,875
Number of feet: 112,175,822.9167
Number of miles: 21,245.421
Number of Empire State Buildings covered by this distance:
   77,203
Number of times you could walk between New York and Paris
   on this line of books: 5.84

Acknowledgments

The Baby-sitters Club was conceived over fifteen years ago, and would not have become a success without dozens and dozens of people who brought their time, energy, vision, and talents to it. To them, I am unendingly grateful. They may never know how much I appreciate them. I want to extend thanks to:

• My editors: Brenda Bowen, my longtime friend, and the first editor on the series; the current editors — Bethany Buck, David Levithan, and Kate Egan (editors extraordinaire); Julie Komorn; Kathryn McKeon; and Janet Vultee.

• The other writers for the Baby-sitters Club, Baby-sitters Little Sister, and California Diaries who, with great sensitivity, shared the voices of Kristy and her friends: Ellen Miles, Peter Lerangis, Stephanie Calmenson, Suzanne Weyn, Nola Thacker, Jahnna Beecham and Malcolm Hillgartner, Gabrielle Charbonnet, Jeanne Betancourt, Jan Carr, Diane Molleson, Vicki Berger Erwin, Mary Lou Kennedy, Helen Perelman, and Laura Dower.

• Hodges Soileau, Susan Tang, Charles Tang, and the other artists whose work brought the characters and their world to life visually.

• David Tommasino, the first art director for the series, and his staff for their insight and vision; Elizabeth Parisi, Dawn Adelman, and Cristina Costantino in the art department; and Holly Tommasino, who created and executed all the handwriting for the characters.

• Ronnie Ambrose, Bonnie Cutler, Annie McDonnell, Laurie Giannelli, Heidi Robinson, Pam LaBarbiera, Nancy Smith, Karyn Browne, and Ellie Berger in production and manufacturing.

The Baby-sitters Club has many other Scholastic friends as well. Among them are Dick Robinson, Barbara Marcus, Ed Monagle, Craig Walker, Judy Newman, Maggie Kniep, Alan Cogen, Betsy Howie, and all those (currently and formerly) in the publicity department, the sales department, the marketing department, the book clubs, and the books fairs who have supported the series.

In addition I would like to thank Adele Brodkin, Lisa Pasquale, Beth Perkins, Debbie Jensen, Madge Christensen, Kirsten Hall, Becca Lieberg, Bonnie Black, Diane Muldrow, and especially Elisa Geliebter for their inestimable help over the years.

As always, I want to thank Laura Godwin.

And most of all, I want to thank Jean Feiwel, who came up with the idea for the Baby-sitters Club and who guided it from the very beginning to the very end. Without her, the series wouldn't have happened at all.

Thank you, Jean.

Check out what's new with your old friends.

☐ BDI 0-590-50391-X	BSC Friends Forever Special: Everything Changes	**$4.50 US each!**
☐ BDI 0-590-52313-9	#1: Kristy's Big News	
☐ BDI 0-590-52318-X	#2: Stacey vs. Claudia	
☐ BDI 0-590-52326-0	#3: Mary Anne's Big Breakup	
☐ BDI 0-590-52331-4	#4: Claudia and the Friendship Feud	
☐ BDI 0-590-52332-5	#5: Kristy Power!	
☐ BDI 0-590-52337-6	#6: Stacey and the Boyfriend Trap	
☐ BDI 0-590-52337-6	#7: Claudia Gets Her Guy	
☐ BDI 0-590-52340-4	#8: Mary Anne's Revenge	
☐ BDI 0-590-52343-0	#9: Kristy and the Kidnapper	
☐ BDI 0-590-52345-7	#10: Stacey's Problem	
☐ BDI 0-590-52346-5	#11: Welcome Home, Mary Anne	
☐ BDI 0-590-52348-1	#12: Claudia and the Disaster Date	

Scholastic Inc., P.O. Box 7502, Jefferson City, MO 65102

Please send me the books I have checked above. I am enclosing $_____ (please add $2.00 to cover shipping and handling). Send check or money order–no cash or C.O.D.s please.

Name_____Birth date_____

Address_____

City_____State/Zip_____

Please allow four to six weeks for delivery. Offer good in U.S.A. only. Sorry, mail orders are not available to residents of Canada. Prices subject to change.